C0-DUO-780

HEART
of
STONE
ARI McKAY

Dreamspinner Press

Published by
Dreamspinner Press
5032 Capital Circle SW
Ste 2, PMB# 279
Tallahassee, FL 32305-7886
USA
http://www.dreamspinnerpress.com/

This is a work of fiction. Names, characters, places, and incidents either are the product of the author's imagination or are used fictitiously, and any resemblance to actual persons, living or dead, business establishments, events, or locales is entirely coincidental.

Heart of Stone
Copyright © 2013 by Ari McKay

Cover Art by Reese Dante
http://www.reesedante.com

Cover content is being used for illustrative purposes only
and any person depicted on the cover is a model.

All rights reserved. No part of this book may be reproduced or transmitted in any form or by any means, electronic or mechanical, including photocopying, recording, or by any information storage and retrieval system without the written permission of the Publisher, except where permitted by law. To request permission and all other inquiries, contact Dreamspinner Press, 5032 Capital Circle SW, Ste 2, PMB# 279, Tallahassee, FL 32305-7886, USA. http://www.dreamspinnerpress.com/

ISBN: 978-1-62380-598-2
Digital ISBN: 978-1-62380-599-9

Printed in the United States of America
First Edition
June 2013

1

"STONE! Hey, Stone! You came back!"

Stone stopped in the middle of uncinching Raider's saddle and glanced up to find Little Sam coming toward him, pushing his way through the press of cowboys and horses crowding the stable. The young man's face was split with a wide grin, and Stone answered it with a slight, tired smile of his own. Little Sam had been laid up with a broken leg when Stone and the other hands had left Yellow Knife, Texas, for Abilene two and a half months before, and no doubt he wanted to hear all about the cattle drive he'd missed, but Stone was too tired to talk much. Unfortunately, that didn't deter the younger man, who followed him into the stall.

"'Course I came back. Why wouldn't I?" Stone asked as he draped his saddle over the stall door and turned back to remove Raider's blanket.

"Well, you were talkin' about stayin' in Kansas before you left." Sam picked up a brush and began to work on Raider's pale golden coat. "I thought maybe you meant it."

Stone shrugged. He *had* thought about it, but Abilene hadn't seemed all that different from Yellow Knife—or San Antonio, Santa Fe, or Tucson, for that matter. He'd been slowly working his way east for the last ten years, but no matter where he went, it still didn't feel like home. He was beginning to think no place ever would.

Sam was watching him, pale blue eyes alight with curiosity, and Stone knew he would have to answer. He didn't make friends easily, but Little Sam had attached himself to Stone from the moment Stone had arrived on the Circle J a bit over a year before, seeming to view Stone as an older brother. Sam was barely twenty and full of energy, with sandy hair, innocent eyes, and a puppy-like enthusiasm for everything that made him a favorite with all the hands. Cutting him off was more than Stone, who had a reputation for being as cold and silent as his name, could manage.

"Changed my mind," he said. "Kansas ain't no better'n here. We made it in good time, didn't lose too many head, and Stevenson got a good price at market, so we all got a bonus. I reckon I could stay on another year."

Sam nodded. Driving cattle from southern Texas to the railhead market in Kansas could be profitable or disastrous, depending as it did on factors like weather, the health of the cattle, the quality of the grazing, and whether or not they ran into rustlers. Jim Stevenson, the owner of the Circle J, drove five thousand head of Texas Longhorns along the Chisholm Trail every year, and mostly he made money at it, but some years were much better than others. Fortunately for Stone and the other hands, this year had been a good one.

"Glad to hear it." Sam grinned at him again. "You got to tell me all about the drive. But first, there's news here, too. For you."

"What?" Stone blinked in surprise, and then he frowned. He didn't like the sound of that; he was of no importance to anyone, and that was the way he preferred it.

"It ain't bad." Sam bit his lip. "Or at least, I don't reckon it's bad. You got a letter, that's all. Got here a couple of weeks after you left. Ms. Stevenson said she figured she'd keep it in case you came back with the others, and if not, she'd send it on to Abilene after you. Looks like it already got sent on a few times anyway." He looked envious. "A real letter! I ain't never got a letter in my life. Who could be writin' you?"

"No idea," Stone replied. He'd never gotten a letter before, either. Why would he? There wasn't anyone to write to him; his mother was dead, and he didn't have anyone else, no friends or family but his horse. He was curious, but it was tinged with dread; surely it could only be bad news, if it had followed him who knew how far. When he moved on, he always told the foreman where he was headed and left on good terms, but that only made sense, because a man never knew what might happen. Stone might not have friends, but he tried not to make enemies, either. "It's waited this long, I suppose it can wait until I get Raider settled."

"Sure." Sam looked disappointed, but then he grinned. "Look, I'll get water and feed for him so you can finish curryin', okay?"

No doubt Sam was hoping Stone would let him see the letter—not read it, but just see what it looked like—in return for the help, and Stone nodded as Sam scurried off. At least the boy hadn't suggested Stone leave off dealing with his horse until after picking up the letter. Anyone with any sense knew a cowboy's horse came before anything else.

"Who in tarnation would write to me?" he muttered, and Raider twitched his ears.

With Sam's help, Stone finished taking care of Raider, but instead of heading to the bunkhouse with the other hands, he made his way to the large, neat timber house where Mr. and Mrs. Stevenson, the ranch's owners and his employers, lived. He removed his hat and knocked on the back door.

Mrs. Stevenson, a kind, sturdy woman in her fifties with iron-gray hair and a plump figure, opened the door. "Why hello, Stone! Glad to see you came back. I reckon Sam told you about the letter, eh? You'd have thought it was for him, the way he's been carryin' on about it. Come in, and I'll fetch it for you."

Stone stepped into the kitchen, which was clean and tidy and smelled wonderfully of baking bread. "I'll just stay by the door, ma'am." He looked down at his dirty boots. "I don't want to track all over your floor."

"All right," she replied and then bustled out of the room. A few moments later, she was back, holding an envelope of brown paper that had writing all over the front. She handed it to him, shaking her head. "Looks like someone really wanted to get ahold of you. It's been forwarded twice from the first address."

"Huh." Stone took it, looking at the front. It had originally been sent to the Lone Pine Ranch in Oklahoma, where he'd been working two years before, and they'd sent it on to the Cut Notch, his last place before he'd come to work for the Stevensons. He supposed it was a good thing he'd told them where he'd been headed or the letter would never have reached him at all. "Thank you, ma'am. I'm much obliged to you for holdin' it for me."

"Pshaw, it wasn't a problem, Stone." Mrs. Stevenson smiled and patted his arm in a motherly fashion. "You're a good worker and a good man. I'm glad you didn't stay in Abilene."

"Thank you, ma'am." Stone felt his neck heating at the compliment. For some reason, praise always embarrassed him, and he shifted his weight from foot to foot. "Er, if you'll excuse me, ma'am, I should be goin'."

"Of course," she replied, shooing him toward the door. Then she paused. "And Stone, if that letter has somethin' that you need help with, let me know. You've got friends here."

"Much obliged." Stone turned and left the cozy kitchen. Now that he had the letter in his hand, he was burning with curiosity. And there was only one way to satisfy it.

2

MAY 14, 1887
   Barrow and Morgan, Attorneys-at-Law
   47 Main Street
   Reno, Nevada

   Dear Mr. Harrison,
   We represent the estate of your late aunt, Mrs. Priscilla Ann Harrison Rivers, who passed away on April 30th. As Mrs. Rivers had no children of her own, her will stipulated that all her worldly possessions were to pass to you as her only living relative. This makes you the sole owner of the Copper Lake Ranch in Washoe County, Nevada.

   As Mrs. Rivers was uncertain of your whereabouts, she made plans before her death for the ranch to be held for you for a period of one year, the taxes and salaries of her employees paid, and an overseer left in charge to allow the ranch to continue to function while we attempted to find you. If you would please send a telegram to our office as soon as you are in receipt of this letter, we will begin to make arrangements to transfer the ranch to your ownership.

   Sincerely,
   Stephen Barrow, Esq.

For several minutes, all Stone could do was stare at the letter, unable to fully understand its meaning. An aunt? He'd barely known his father, remembering him only as an angry man who drank and hit both him and his mother; he certainly hadn't known his father had any family, much less someone who owned a ranch and who would actually leave it to Stone, a man she'd never met. It made him wonder why his mother never said anything, although given her fear of the man she'd married, and her relief when he'd gotten himself killed in a fall from a horse, it was possible she hadn't wanted anything more to do with his family.

The letter was dated five months before, and given the distance from Nevada to Texas, Stone was amazed it had found him before the one year deadline. Which meant he had a decision to make: did he want to claim this unexpected inheritance, or just pretend the letter hadn't reached him and let the ranch go to whoever next stood to inherit?

He folded the letter and slipped it into the pocket of his jacket, then stared out across the dusty expanse of one of Circle J's pastures, empty except for a few of the breeding cows that would provide the stock for next year's market. The ranch was huge, and Stone knew that he, as a hand, saw only a small part of what it took to keep the place running. Mr. Stevenson and his foreman, Ben, worked hard every day and were responsible for every person and animal on the ranch. If there was a bad year, a cowboy could always move along to greener pastures, especially ones like Stone who didn't have a family. But Mr. Stevenson had invested his whole life in this one place. If things went bad, he couldn't just move on to the next place, the next job. He had to stay and do his best, no matter how bad it got.

Of course, his father hadn't taught him that. Paul Harrison hadn't taken responsibility for anything in his life. Everything had always been someone else's fault, especially his half-Indian wife's. Stone couldn't remember a time in his life when he'd ever looked at his father with anything but fear and hatred, even though his mother had tried to make apologies for his father's behavior. Perhaps she had even begun to feel as though she deserved the scathing words and the blows, after so many years of hearing how Paul Harrison could have been someone if only he hadn't had a half-breed wife and son to tie him down.

That hadn't kept Paul from hauling the two of them from town to town, always looking for a way to make easy money. People had called his father no-account and shiftless, claiming he'd never done an honest day's work in his life, and Stone could believe it was true. He'd been less than ten years old when his father died, and he couldn't remember feeling anything but relief when it happened. From that moment on, he'd done everything in his power to prove he was nothing like his father. He'd taken care of his mother, gone to school, and worked hard at any job he could get to help them survive. He never wanted people to look at him the way they looked at his father. He did an honest day's work for an honest day's pay, and even though he'd not stayed on any one ranch for more than a couple of years, he always moved on in a way that left good feelings behind him.

Over the years he'd encountered plenty of people who didn't like him, mostly because of the color of his skin, but he'd dealt with it, and for the most part, he felt good about himself. He was a good cowboy, but could he handle running a ranch of his own? Did he even want to try? How would he feel if he failed?

If there was one thing he'd learned about himself over the years, it was that he'd pretty much always tried to do things exactly opposite the way his father would have done them. Which meant accepting the responsibilities he was given and doing his very best to fulfill them. Now someone was entrusting him with a ranch. He didn't know if it was a prosperous place or a rundown spread on the verge of collapse, but in his heart, he knew it didn't matter. An aunt he'd never known had seen fit to entrust her place to him, despite the fact she must have known he could have turned out just like his father. She'd given him a responsibility, and Stone knew what he had to do: make every attempt to be successful at it.

Exactly the way his father wouldn't have done.

3

"WELL, I'll be damned."

Stone pulled Raider to a stop, and stared at the sight in front of him. The mountains in the distance were breathtaking, but he'd seen them on the horizon since he'd arrived in Reno two days before. They'd gotten closer as he'd ridden southwest, and the terrain had become gently rolling foothills covered in luxurious green. As he'd crested a particularly high hill, he came upon a valley stretched out before him, containing a large lake of the most incredible, unearthly blue he'd ever seen in his life. It was positively dazzling in the sunlight, and he couldn't move for a moment, struck by the beauty of it and an almost overwhelming wish that his mother could have lived to see it.

This, then, was Copper Lake, and the neat buildings perched on the shore must be Copper Lake Ranch. According to the papers in his saddlebags, his ranch was a spread of nearly ten thousand acres with upwards of eight thousand head of cattle. It still didn't seem quite real to him, but Stone knew what he had to do. He clicked to Raider, and the horse started forward again. He figured he'd best get down there and introduce himself so he could get a start on taking care of what needed to be done.

Twenty minutes later, he dismounted in front of the ranch house. It was a solid wood and stone building, and it had been around a while, for it had a mellow, weathered look that new buildings couldn't match.

He slipped the reins around a post and started up the steps, hoping someone was home. He couldn't hear any movement, but he knocked on the door and belatedly snatched off his hat and held it in his hands as he waited to see if someone would answer.

He heard the familiar sound of boot steps on a hardwood floor, growing louder as they approached, and then the door opened, and Stone was staring into a pair of pale blue eyes.

"Can I help you?" The man's voice was a deep, lazy drawl, a good match for his relaxed posture. He looked to be a couple of inches shorter than Stone and maybe a few years older, and his light brown hair was cut short and neat. His face and hands were tanned, but Stone was willing to bet he was lily white where the sun didn't shine.

"My name is Stone Harrison." He drew in a deep breath, willing himself to not show any nervousness. "I'm Mrs. Rivers' nephew, and she left the ranch to me."

"Well, it's mighty nice to meet you, Mr. Harrison. We've been hopin' you'd turn up." The man smiled and held out his hand. "I'm Luke Reynolds. I'm... I *was* Priss's foreman."

Stone took the man's hand, and his eyes widened as he felt a tingle at the contact of their palms. He shook quickly and released, softening the abruptness with a brief, small smile.

"Pleased to meet you," he said politely, knowing that things would be much easier if this man was on his side and inclined to help him. "To be honest, Mr. Reynolds, I'd be much obliged if you'd still consider yourself foreman here. A week ago, I weren't nothin' but a hand myself. I don't know if Mrs. Rivers would have left this place to me if she'd known I've got no experience runnin' a spread."

Luke nodded, his smile widening as if the offer pleased him, and he held the door open, stepping aside in a clear invitation. "I'd be glad to stay on. Truth is, I've been here so long, I wouldn't know where to go anyways."

Relieved things were so far going so well—after all, he could have been met with a shotgun and an invitation to leave—Stone crossed the threshold. The house was as neat inside as out, and even bigger than the Stevensons' had been.

"Sounds like we'll make a good team then," he replied, fervently hoping it would be true. He was feeling out of his depth, but he couldn't let it show. "I suppose you can tell me what needs doin'? The lawyers in Reno knew even less about ranchin' than I did, and they wanted to talk in whys and wherefores till my head was spinnin'."

"Oh sure." Luke nodded amiably. "I was practically runnin' the place anyway. I had to," he added, glancing at Stone as he led the way into the parlor. "Priss was too sick to do it herself that last year or two, so she started trainin' me up."

The parlor was a far more comfortable room than Stone expected it to be, devoid of fussy little antimacassars and delicate china figurines like he'd seen in so many parlors. The furniture was sturdy and made of dark wood. The sofa looked to be made of leather, and the chairs were upholstered in thick brocade. A floor-to-ceiling bookshelf took up most of one wall, and there was also a rolltop writing desk that looked neatly organized.

"Have a seat." Luke gestured toward the sofa. "Can I get you somethin'?"

"I'd appreciate some water, if it ain't an imposition." Stone settled down gingerly on the sofa. He was surprised at how casually Mr. Reynolds referred to his aunt, but then again, they'd probably been close if she'd been so sick she'd had to turn her duties over to her foreman.

"Sure thing, Mr. Harrison." Luke smiled at him again, and Stone thought perhaps Luke's gaze lingered a little longer than it ought to before he sauntered out of the room. He returned a few minutes later with a tall glass of water, so cold Stone could see condensation beading on the sides. "Straight from the well out back," Luke explained as he handed over the glass. "This close to the mountains, the water underground is right cold all year round."

"Much obliged," Stone replied, taking the glass and sipping gratefully, appreciating its coolness, as well as the distraction it gave him. He wasn't a talkative man by nature, and he was feeling as out of place as a turkey in a henhouse. Part of him wondered if it was too late to forget the whole thing and head back to Yellow Knife, but he'd never run out on anything in his life, so he was just going to have to tighten his belt and deal with it.

Lowering the glass, he turned to Mr. Reynolds. "So how about you have a seat and tell me what I've gotten myself into?"

Luke claimed one of the chairs, settling in with more apparent ease than Stone felt, stretching his long legs out in front of him and crossing them at the ankle. "What you've got, Mr. Harrison, is a right large chunk of land that's doin' well for itself. If you've got half the sense your aunt had in runnin' this place, you'll be set for life."

Stone thought about that for a minute and nodded. "Well, I'm plannin' to give it a try." The thought of his father crossed his mind again, making him scowl. "And call me Stone. Don't know how much sense my aunt had, but I reckon it must have been a fair bit to have kept this place so nice. Hope I've got enough not to mess that up."

"You can call me Luke, and I hope you don't mess it up, too." There was a mischievous twinkle in Luke's eyes that suggested he was teasing. "Don't worry, I'll teach you what you need to know."

"All right, Luke." The teasing took Stone by surprise and he wasn't certain how to respond. No one had ever teased him but his mother, and that had been a long time ago. "Why don't you start by tellin' me who all is around the ranch?" He grimaced. "I suppose I'm goin' to have to talk to a lot of people."

"Or you could make me talk to them." Luke said easily. "Yeah, you need to learn who's who if you're goin' to be in charge, but if you want to delegate somethin' to me, well, that's what a foreman is for."

Stone frowned. He didn't know Luke at all, so he couldn't be sure if he could take the offer at face value or not. Maybe his aunt had let Luke do what he wanted around the place, and now Luke didn't want a new owner coming in and having ideas of his own. Whatever the reason, Stone felt his hackles rising.

11

"I don't have nothin' else to do but learn how to do this job." Stone lifted his chin and looked Luke squarely in the eye. "I don't know what Mrs. Rivers may have told you about my pa, but she sure didn't know me, and I ain't nothin' like he was."

Luke raised both hands in an attitude of surrender. "I ain't got no ideas about you or your pa. Priss didn't much like talkin' about her brother, and she never said nothin' about you. If you do right by this ranch and the people who work here, you and me won't have any problems. I just don't want to see all her hard work go to ruin, that's all."

Stone set his jaw stubbornly. Maybe his aunt hadn't talked much about her no-account brother to Luke, but that didn't mean people didn't know, since presumably Paul Harrison had grown up here, same as his sister. "I know all about hard work. And I'd rather give this ranch to someone else than wreck it. I treat other folks like I want to be treated, so if that's doin' right by them in your opinion, we should get along all right."

"So we should," Luke agreed, appearing unruffled by Stone's prickliness. If anything, he seemed amused by their conversation. "I reckon it's a bit late in the day for a tour, but I can start showin' you around first thing in the mornin'. This is your place now, so you can have Priss' old room if you want it."

That gave Stone pause; he'd not really thought about the fact that he'd be living in the ranch house, not out in the bunkhouse. But the thought of staying in the room of a woman, one he'd never met to boot, didn't set well with him, and he shifted uncomfortably. "Is there another room?" He lowered his gaze. "I sure don't need nothin' fancy or big."

Luke nodded. "There's a guest bedroom. We don't get a lot of guests anyway, and we can turn Priss' room into the guest bedroom if you'd rather, or there's Sarah's old room. She was the housekeeper. You can have either of those, if that suits you better."

"The guest bedroom would be fine." Stone looked at Luke with a frown. "There's no housekeeper here now?" He gestured at the room, which was clean and didn't seem to be dusty or cluttered. "Who takes care of the place, then? I sure don't know nothin' about cleanin' up a place this big."

"Well, I do look right pretty in a ruffled apron," Luke drawled, and then he laughed at the look on Stone's face. "Naw, after Sarah left, I hired a girl from town to come in and do the cookin', cleanin', and washin', but she leaves when she's done for the day."

Apparently Luke was a bit of a joker, and Stone sighed quietly, telling himself he was just going to have to put up with it, since he needed Luke's help. "Well if that suits you, it's fine with me." Something occurred to him, and he regarded Luke questioningly. "Does that mean you live in this house, too?"

"Indeed I do," Luke affirmed. "I worked for Miss Priss a long time, and we got to be close. Almost like family, you might say. She stopped treatin' me like just a foreman a while back, and when she got sick, me being right here in the house made helpin' Sarah take care of her a lot easier."

"Makes sense." Stone nodded. It was unusual for the foreman to stay in the main house, but his aunt hadn't had any family to take care of her, so Luke had stepped in, which was nice of him. "Well, it's a big place, and I've been livin' in bunkhouses for the last ten years, so if you want to stay here, it won't bother me. Although...." He paused, knowing that his neck was probably turning red, but he needed to get it out in the open. "If you want to do any courtin', I'd be obliged if you'd do it at the foreman's house."

Luke laughed, although Stone couldn't see what was so funny. It was almost like Luke was amused by a joke only he knew. "I ain't of a mind to go courtin'." He was still smiling, although Stone didn't get the impression Luke was making fun of him. "None of the girls 'round here interest me much."

"All right." Stone wondered what Luke meant, but he wasn't going to ask, taking his words at face value instead. Apparently Luke was picky about his women, which was fine with Stone. He had no use for women whatsoever, at least not in the way men usually did. Not that he wanted anyone to know that; information like that getting out could ruin a man's life, and Stone had enough to deal with just being part Indian. He stood up, deciding he'd had enough small talk for one night. "Well, then, I suppose I ought to get my horse taken care of and then find somethin' to eat before bed."

Luke rose as well. "There's some cold fried chicken and cornbread in the kitchen. I'm willin' to bet there's pie, too. Mary always leaves too much for my supper, and I don't mind sharin'."

"Thanks, I'd appreciate that." Stone loosened up enough to smile. Fried chicken and pie sounded like heaven, since he'd eaten nothing but cold bread and beans that morning in his hurry to get to the ranch. "But Raider comes first."

"Of course." Luke nodded, as if Stone's attitude was the most sensible thing in the world, which set Stone's mind more at ease. The man understood the importance of a good horse, at least. "There's plenty of empty stalls, so take whichever one you want. I'll dish up the food. Just come on back to the kitchen when you're done."

"All right, thanks." Stone walked through the parlor and out the front door. It felt odd, seeing himself out that way, but that's what you did in your own place. He hadn't had a place to call his own in a very long time, and he hadn't even realized how much he missed it until he stood there on the wide porch of the ranch house, looking out over the serene blue water of Copper Lake and missing his mother with a soul-deep ache. He was a loner by nature, but even loners could want a place to call their own. Somehow this place felt right to him, as though he could actually belong. As though he could make it a home.

Raider saw him and snorted, and Stone wasted no time jamming his hat back on his head. "I'm comin'. I ain't forgot you." He hurried down the stairs and patted the horse fondly on the nose. "Let's go see if your new place is as nice as mine seems to be."

Indeed, the barn behind the house was large and well stocked, and Stone found everything he needed to make his horse comfortable. He couldn't resist a peek in the other stalls, with a cowboy's innate interest in good horseflesh. There were over thirty stalls in the barn, all of them empty except for three, which meant the men hadn't come back from the day's work yet.

One stall held a beautiful, pregnant gray mare with the softest eyes Stone had ever seen, and she whinnied to him until he stroked her on the nose. "Hey, girl, you're a pretty thing." She agreed, apparently, and nudged him pointedly until he chuckled and got an apple for her out of a nearby bushel basket.

The other horses were another gray mare, as pretty as the first one, and a big, strong plow horse, who looked him over but didn't seem ready to make friends just yet. Curiosity satisfied for the moment, Stone made his way back to the house, going to the back door where he was pretty certain the kitchen would be. He was right, and he dumped his saddlebags by the door as he looked around. It was a big room, bright and cheerful, and he liked it.

"This is a well-kept place," he said to Luke, as he crossed to the sink to wash up. "It's good to see."

"Priss was particular about doin' things right." Luke carried two loaded plates to the table. In addition to the promised chicken and cornbread, mashed potatoes were piled high, slathered in white gravy, and Stone's stomach growled again when Luke set it in front of him. "She was proud of this place and determined to show everyone she could run it herself. I did things her way from the beginnin', and now they're my way, too."

Stone picked up his fork. "Makes sense." He paused, suddenly self-conscious. He wasn't a religious man, but maybe Luke was, so he waited to see what Luke did.

Luke bent his head and said grace, keeping it brief, and then he nodded at Stone. "Dig in. There's more chicken if you want it."

"Thanks." Stone did so, enjoying the taste of fresh, home cooked food. He'd have to compliment Mary on her cooking when he met her and make sure she wanted to stick around.

Luke's appetite didn't seem to be lacking either, and he enjoyed the meal as much as Stone. Fortunately, he didn't make small talk while they ate.

15

"That was good." Stone gave a sigh of contentment as he polished off the last bite. "I was hungrier than I thought." He rose, picking up his plate and carrying it to the sink. "I'll wash up, since you were nice enough to share your supper with me."

Leaning back in his chair, Luke regarded Stone inquisitively. "You're the boss," he pointed out. "You don't have to do the washin' up if you don't want to."

"As I said, I don't mind cleanin' up after myself. Been doin' it for a long time." Stone crossed to the table and pointed to Luke's empty plate. "If you're done, can I take that?"

"Sure enough, if you're set on washin' up anyway." Luke picked up his plate and handed it over, the surprise in his expression shifting into what appeared to be approval.

Stone took the plate, and then he carefully washed everything, stacking it next to the sink and drying it with a towel that was dangling from a hook on the pantry cabinet. He wasn't certain where everything got put away, so he left it; better to let Mary or Luke put things where they belonged.

After washing and drying his hands, he turned to Luke. He wasn't much for socializing, and he found himself suddenly bone-weary. "If it's all the same to you, I think I'll call it an early night." He paused, wondering if that sounded weak or if Luke would think he was soft or something. "I'd just got back from a ten-week cattle drive when I got the letter last week, and I've been on the move ever since, tryin' to get here. I think it's catchin' up with me."

"I ain't been a foreman so long that I've forgotten what it's like," Luke said, sounding sympathetic, as if he really did understand, and he pushed back his chair and rose. "C'mon, I'll show you to your room, and you can get settled. Tomorrow, I'll show you around. Mary has breakfast on the table by six, and we can leave right after."

"Sounds fine." Stone was glad Luke didn't seem to think badly of him. Now that he'd eaten, all he could think about was climbing into bed and getting some much-needed shut-eye. He picked up his saddlebags. "Ready when you are."

Luke led him upstairs to a bedroom that wasn't grand, like the master bedroom likely would be, but it was spacious enough for him. It was furnished only with a bed, a wardrobe, a washstand, and a small bedside table, with lace curtains at the window and a colorful quilt on the bed.

"Here you go." Luke smiled as he waved Stone inside. "It's all yours. If you need anything, I'm right next door."

"This is just fine. Thanks again for supper."

"Night, boss." Luke waved cheerfully and sauntered away, going downstairs. Stone watched him go, and then he closed the door with a shake of his head. Luke was one of those sociable people who always perplexed him; he just didn't understand actually *liking* being around other people. But as Luke had said, he was the boss, which meant he only had to be sociable if he wanted to.

The sun was setting, but Stone didn't bother to light the lamp on the table. Instead he stripped and crawled between the sheets, settling down on the firm mattress with a sigh. He barely had time to think about what he was going to have to do the next day before he fell quickly and deeply asleep.

17

4

AS THEY rode along at a leisurely pace, Luke took the opportunity to study his new boss without getting distracted by the fact that Stone Harrison was a handsome devil. He'd felt a jolt of attraction and awareness as soon as they'd shaken hands, but he'd tried to ignore it, reminding himself Stone probably didn't share his inclinations.

Still, that didn't keep him from admiring the view. Tall and long-legged with jet black hair, dark eyes, and tanned skin, Stone was just the type to set Luke ablaze, and unless Luke missed his guess, Stone had a little Indian blood in him somewhere. Those high cheekbones were as much a clue as his dark hair and skin, but Luke didn't care if he did or didn't. Luke didn't hate Indians or fear them like some white folk did. They were just people like any other, and he thought Stone was one of the best-looking men he'd ever seen, no matter who begot him.

Looking was all he could do, however, and so he behaved himself while he showed Stone around the ranch, starting with the house grounds. Before they left the house, he'd showed off their indoor plumbing and icebox with pride; Priss had been able to afford a few comforts, and she hadn't been so thrifty she'd deprived herself of them. He'd introduced Stone to the thirty-odd hands, most of whom would be with them through the winter, and he'd taken Stone around to the barn, the hay sheds, and the main stock area, and then they'd mounted up to see some of the pasture area, the lake, and the copper mine.

Flanked by the mountains, the ranch was as beautiful as it was productive, at least as far as Luke was concerned. He'd been there nigh on ten years, and he still wasn't weary of the view. He couldn't tell by looking at his profile whether Stone appreciated it too, and since they had a few miles to go with only themselves for company, he decided to start up a little conversation.

"So what do you think?" he asked casually. "Like what you see so far?"

Stone turned his head toward Luke, his dark eyes gleaming. For the most part, Stone had a damned good poker face, one that betrayed little of what he was thinking, but there was no mistaking the light of pride and possession in his gaze. Luke had seen it in Priss's eyes often enough, and it looked likely the deep connection she'd shared with the ranch had been transferred in full measure to the nephew she'd never met.

"Yes." Stone's voice was soft, his tone almost reverent. "I like it a lot."

"Good. Me too," Luke replied with a warm smile as he admired the way Stone's face was transformed with his inner light. Stone didn't have to know Luke wasn't talking about just the majestic mountains and rolling pastures, and Luke wasn't about to admit it, but he was starting to think working for Stone was either going to be the best job he'd ever had or the worst, depending on how out of hand this wayward attraction got. Possibly a little of both. "I never get tired of lookin' around when I'm ridin' fence. Seems like there's always somethin' new to see."

Stone nodded, turning his gaze toward the mountains. "I forgot how beautiful it is out here," he murmured, almost to himself. "Sky's so close you could almost touch it." He cleared his throat, as though embarrassed by what he'd said. "It's a lot of fence to ride. Must take a heap of time keepin' it up."

Luke nodded in agreement. "A place this big always has somethin' that needs doin'. You won't never be bored, that's for sure."

That earned him a snort. "I can imagine. Hard work don't worry me. I'd rather be busy anyways."

"That won't be a problem," Luke replied dryly. "No matter how much you pass off to me, you'll have a full plate any time of year." He paused, hoping he didn't sound like he was trying to take over. "And don't worry, I ain't tryin' to tell you what to do or take your place. You're the boss, and I'm the foreman, and I ain't got no mind to switch places. But I don't mind helpin' as much as you want me to."

Stone was quiet for a moment, and then he looked at Luke again. "I appreciate that. Like I said, I don't know much about bein' a boss. Always been content to only worry about myself and my horse." He paused and looked down at the back of Raider's neck. "Guess that needs to change. I won't have folks sayin' I don't try my best, even if I mess up."

"You're goin' to have a lot of people lookin' to you now." Luke hoped he wasn't making the situation sound too dire. "But as long as you're fair and carry your weight, ain't no one goin' to complain." He smiled, deciding it was time to lighten the mood. "Ownin' a big, prosperous spread like this ain't all bad, and it ain't all work all the time. You're goin' to have a lot of the local gals real interested in you now, that's for sure. You could have your pick."

Suddenly Stone reined his horse to a stop, and he looked at Luke with a frown of consternation. "Gals? You mean the ones you don't seem to think are very interestin'?"

Luke stopped as well, uncharacteristically flustered as he tried to figure out how to answer the question without revealing the truth. This ranch was his home now, and he didn't want to be kicked out and lose his job and this place all at once because his new boss wasn't happy about having a foreman who fancied men instead of women.

"Well, just because they don't interest me none don't mean one of them might not strike your fancy," he said at last.

Stone's expression didn't change, but Luke noticed a flush had risen under his tan. "Doubt it. Don't have time for it anyways, if I'm goin' to learn how to run this place."

"Well, one day, you'll have it all figured out, and then you might want to cast your eye around," Luke pointed out, hoping he wasn't inadvertently squelching Stone's social life with all his talk about how busy the ranch would keep them. "I won't even ask you to take your courtin' to one of the outbuildings," he added with a mischievous grin.

For some reason, Stone only turned redder. "You ain't goin' to have to worry about that," he growled, and then he tapped Raider with his heels, spurring the horse into a fast walk.

The reaction puzzled Luke. He wondered if Stone was shy around women or if there was something else going on. A man as handsome as Stone ought to be plenty experienced, not blushing at the mere mention of courting. Unless….

He signaled Mist to speed up as well and caught up to Stone, studying him in silence. Was it possible Stone didn't fancy women either? He wasn't sure, and he couldn't ask outright unless he wanted to risk being punched in the face on top of being fired, but maybe he could find out somehow.

"I guess that means it'll be real quiet around the big house." He kept his tone casual. "Just a couple of bachelors sittin' around together every night."

Stone gave him a sideways glance. "Sounds fine to me. I'm not much for bein' social. Don't need dancin' and drinkin' like some cowboys who don't have no sense."

"You don't have to drink and dance to be social," Luke pointed out. "You can take a lady out for a fancy dinner, a buggy ride, or a picnic." He was fishing, but hopefully not too obviously.

That earned him a flat out scowl, and Stone's jaw clenched. "Maybe I could. If I ever wanted to." His eyes narrowed. "You ain't got a sister you're thinkin' about throwin' at me, do you? I don't hold with fightin', but I just might have to punch you if you try somethin' like that."

21

Luke's eyebrows climbed almost to his hairline at that, and his suspicions grew even stronger at Stone's unusually forceful objections to the idea of courting a woman. This had to be more than mere shyness or lack of experience with women!

"Nothin' like that," he replied easily, deciding it was time to be a little more direct. "I ain't got no family that wants to claim me, if you want the truth. See, they found out I ain't exactly fond of courtin' the ladies either." He fixed Stone with a steady, direct look. "My momma caught me behind the barn with my pants around my ankles, and it weren't no young lady I was with at the time, if you take my meanin'."

"What?" Stone stopped Raider in his tracks again, and the horse gave a whinny of protest at the sudden pull of reins. He stared at Luke, dark eyes wide in a way that would have been funny if the subject hadn't been so serious. He had apparently forgotten how to speak, too, since his mouth opened and closed, but no sound came out. A few moments later, Stone shook himself like a man who'd felt something walk over his grave and cleared his throat.

"I sure hope you was with another man," he said finally, his tone as dry as desert sand. "Because if it was a cow or a horse or some other critter, I think we might have us a problem."

Luke laughed as he guided Mist to stop parallel with Raider, although if he was honest, part of his laughter was born out of sheer relief he wasn't about to be punched, fired, or shot. "No critters." He grinned at Stone. "Just another boy lookin' for a helpin' hand that I was willin' to give."

"Hmmm." The sound Stone made could have meant anything, but there was no condemnation in his eyes. In fact, Luke thought there might even be the tiniest hint of speculation or maybe curiosity. Yet Stone didn't make an admission of his own; instead he simply started forward again, gaze returning to the mountains, and when he finally spoke, his tone was casual, as though he were talking about the weather. "I reckon the rest of the hands don't know, do they?"

"It ain't something I care to have spread around," Luke replied, glancing sidelong at him. "I don't mix business and pleasure, neither. I do my job and leave the hands alone. Anything else is askin' for trouble." He paused, debating on whether he ought to admit the full truth or not, but then, he supposed Stone would hear the rumors for himself the minute he stepped foot into town because all the local gossiping tongues would be happy to have a new ear to wag to. "Truth is, everybody thought me and Priss were sweet on each other, and we let 'em. I did love her, but like a sister, that's all."

"She knew?" Stone looked surprised again, though not as thunderstruck as he had at Luke's original admission. "And she let people think the two of you had goings on?" The red started creeping back up Stone's neck. "But she must have been twenty years older'n you!"

"Well, it helped her, too," Luke drawled, deciding he might as well spill everything and get it over with. "Actually, it helped her and Sarah both to let folks think what they wanted to about us."

"Sarah?" Stone looked perplexed. "The housekeeper? What's she got to do with anything?"

Luke stared at Stone, surprised he hadn't picked up on the implications, and then he chuckled and shook his head, realizing Stone must be more naïve and inexperienced than he'd thought.

"Everything," he replied. "Priss and Sarah loved each other for over twenty years. That's why Sarah couldn't stay when Priss died. It was too painful for her. Too many memories. When I came along, and we realized none of us had the kind of preferences most people would say we ought to have, we agreed to cover for each other. There had been whispers about Priss and Sarah, you see, but those got hushed up right quick when I moved into the big house."

"But my aunt was married!" Stone objected. "What about her husband?"

"It wasn't the same." Luke shook his head. "She only got married because it was what everyone said she ought to do, but it wasn't what she wanted. She loved her husband, but she was in love with Sarah." He paused, thinking about what Priss had gone through in her youth. "It's sad," he mused. "Men can stay single all their lives, and no one thinks badly of them, but women are expected to get married and have babies. We've got it easier in some ways."

"I suppose." Stone seemed distracted, obviously still trying to wrap his mind around everything Luke had told him. Or at least that's what Luke assumed, since it didn't appear Stone even realized what he had just admitted in response to Luke's comment.

Luke hid a triumphant grin, pleased he'd managed to wring the truth out of Stone, even if it was indirectly, and he resisted the urge to make a comment about apples not falling far from trees. "Anyway, don't believe nothin' you hear about Miss Priss and me. Ain't none of it true. She only had eyes for Sarah, and me…." He smiled lazily. "Well, I'm particular about who I tell my secrets to."

That pulled Stone's attention back to him. "Must not be too particular, if you're tellin' your boss." Stone raised a brow. "Not to mention you don't even know me. How do you know I'm not gonna use this against you?" He scowled. "The point of keepin' secrets is so people can't use them to get at you. And you do that by not spillin' them to every man jack what comes along."

"I don't spill them to just everyone," Luke protested. "Just to you. Maybe I'm wrong, but I'm thinkin' you know a little something about keepin' secrets yourself, and I'm thinkin' I can trust you with mine. If you're like your aunt at all, you've got a lot of honor in you, and you won't go around blabbin' just because you can."

Stone looked at him, and then shrugged. "I ain't goin' to blab. Just don't go expectin' me to start tellin' you any secrets I might have. I learned a long time ago that trustin' people don't work out so good."

"Fair enough." Luke briefly considered pointing out that Stone had told him a secret, but considering Stone probably hadn't meant to, he decided to keep it to himself. Drawing attention to Stone's inadvertent admission might make Stone angry and defensive, and Luke didn't want that.

Oh no, he wanted Stone in a more amiable mind, not on guard against him. The more at ease Stone was, the easier it would be for

Luke to wriggle under all those defenses—and if he was lucky, maybe he could wriggle his way right into Stone's bed.

"We're goin' to be workin' together real close, so I reckon we got plenty of time to get to know each other," he added casually. "Maybe one day, you'll even start trustin' me a little bit."

"Maybe." It seemed Stone had reached his limit with personal talk, because he suddenly waved toward the mountains impatiently. "We goin' to chatter all day, or are you goin' to show me that copper mine?"

"I'll be glad to show you whatever you've got a mind to see, boss." Luke was unable to resist teasing a little even though he doubted Stone would pick up on it. "If we pick up the pace, we can be there in about an hour."

"Fine." With that, Stone kicked Raider up to a trot, too fast for easy conversation.

Chuckling quietly to himself, Luke guided Mist to a fast trot as well, keeping a little distance between him and Stone. He could tell seducing Stone was going to be akin to taming a skittish horse, which meant he'd need a lot of patience. Slow and steady would do it, and Luke had nothing but time. Somehow, he already knew Stone would be worth the effort.

5

STONE stared nervously at his reflection in the glass and adjusted his bolo tie. He had bathed, and his dark hair was still damp, but he'd combed it neatly. His clothes were clean, thanks to Mary, but nothing could be done about the fact that they were pretty old and had been mended over the years. Still, it was the best he could do, at least for the moment, since he'd been a simple cowboy only a week ago, and they'd been good enough then. Maybe they'd be good enough, he hoped, for the church-going people of the little town of Serenity, Nevada.

Stone wasn't a religious man. It wasn't that he didn't believe in a higher power, but he'd seen too much violence between the whites and his mother's people over religion to know exactly what he should believe. But he didn't want to be the subject of gossip, so he went to church like everyone else. It was just easier that way.

He picked up his hat and left the bedroom, heading down the stairs toward the kitchen. Mary had the day off, but there was plenty of food in the kitchen for breakfast, if he could manage to eat anything with the way the butterflies were fluttering around in his stomach. He never liked being in a crowd of people he didn't know, not when he was hiding things about himself he knew would make some people want to string him up on the nearest tree.

Entering the kitchen, he put his hat on the table and went to the icebox, deciding that ham and toast might be something he could get down.

A few minutes later, Luke sauntered into the kitchen, looking quite different than usual; he was wearing a blue serge suit with a crisp, white shirt and a bolo tie, and his light brown hair was damp and neatly combed. His strong jaw was clean-shaven with nary a hint of stubble, and his dress boots were shined to the point of gleaming.

"Mornin', boss," he drawled, offering Stone a friendly smile. "Want me to make some coffee?"

Stone went still, arrested by the sight of Luke looking so different. He'd not wanted to admit to himself that, since Luke's admission about his preferences, he'd been noticing just how handsome Luke was, but it was even harder to ignore now. Damn it.

He didn't want Luke to get the wrong idea, so he nodded. "Please." He gestured to the bread he was slicing. "Want some toast?"

"If you're fixin' it, I'll sure eat it." Luke flashed a playful grin at him. For whatever reason, Luke seemed to enjoy teasing him, although it never seemed mean-spirited. Stone got the feeling Luke was trying to make him laugh or smile for some reason, which perplexed him. People tended to leave him be once they realized he wasn't much of a talker and preferred to be by himself.

He nodded, cutting a few more slices of bread and putting them in the toasting rack before sliding it into the oven of the big iron stove. He forked another piece of ham into the skillet, and then he moved out of the way so Luke could put the coffee pot on.

Despite his effort to get out of the way, Luke's arm grazed against his, their shoulders brushing, although Luke didn't seem to notice as he prepared the coffee pot. He doubted Luke even realized he was crowding Stone's space, but Stone could smell the shaving soap Luke used, and suddenly the kitchen seemed very small.

"'Scuse me," Stone said, taking a step back. He'd just wait until Luke moved away before dealing with the rest of the food.

Luke gave him an ingenuous look. "Am I in your way? Sorry, boss, I don't mean to crowd you, but I reckon there's plenty of room over here for both of us."

Stone looked at him narrowly. Sometimes he couldn't tell when Luke was joking and when he was being serious, which kept him off balance. He'd known a lot of cowboys, but he'd never met anyone quite like Luke, and he wasn't quite sure how to act in return.

He shrugged. "'S okay. But you're goin' to have to move so I can open the door and get the toast before it burns."

"Sure thing, boss." Luke's smile didn't seem quite appropriate for Sunday morning as he looked at Stone with a wicked gleam in his eyes, and he moved just enough to let Stone by, standing with his hip cocked and right at eye level when Stone bent to open the oven door.

Stone retrieved the toast and straightened, looking down at Luke and keeping his expression carefully neutral. "You're awfully cheerful for a man who ain't had coffee yet. I'm not so cheerful. Might be safer to remember that."

"Will do, boss." Luke seemed unperturbed as he turned his attention back to the coffee, remaining quiet until it was done, and he offered Stone a generously filled cup, prepared just the way he liked it. "Maybe you'll be a little more cheerful after this."

Stone filled his plate with buttered toast and a slice of ham, and then he took the cup. "Thanks," he replied, moving to the table and taking the seat, which after a week already felt like "his." He sipped the coffee and glanced at Luke, watching as he got his plate and took the seat across the table.

There were things about the foreman Stone found unsettling. There was no denying the man was a hard worker, and he knew everything about how to run a ranch as big as Copper Lake, but he seemed determined to keep Stone flustered, which, unfortunately, he seemed to find easy to do. Stone wasn't used to being teased, and while he didn't think Luke meant it in a hurtful way, he simply didn't know how to respond most of the time. Especially when the way Luke's lips curled up when he smiled was beginning to become all too distracting, which only made Stone feel more out of his depth. But he couldn't deny he needed Luke around, so he would have to put up with the man somehow.

He finished his coffee, then rose and went to fetch the pot from the stove to refill his cup. "More?" He raised the pot and looked at Luke.

"Might as well," Luke replied, holding out his cup. "I might need it. Our preacher ain't the most soul-stirrin' of men in the pulpit."

"Oh?" Stone poured carefully so as not to spill it over Luke's hand and burn him. "Well, can't say as I've heard many who are."

Luke chuckled, and his eyes were warm as he gazed up at Stone. "Neither have I, but Miss Priss was always big on doin' the right thing, and that included showin' up at church on Sunday mornin'. If it was up to me, I'd probably stop, but somehow, I can't bring myself to go against what I know she'd want."

Stone put the pot back on the stove, then pulled out his pocket watch, pleased to see they had plenty of time before they needed to leave. If what Luke said was true, he'd need the second cup of coffee, too.

"Well, doin' the right thing makes sense." He took his seat again, stretching his legs out comfortably underneath the table. "Especially if you don't want to give folk reason to look too closely at other parts of your life. Seems to me a lot of time people see what they want to see."

"That they do." Luke nodded. "That's what Priss, Sarah, and I counted on, as a matter of fact."

Stone looked at Luke over the rim of his cup. It appeared Luke had found an almost perfect situation for himself, and he seemed comfortable with himself in a way Stone envied. Luke didn't seem to live in fear of having his secrets discovered, which was almost beyond Stone's comprehension. He'd lived with the feeling of having to look over his shoulder for so long, he wasn't sure he'd ever be able to completely relax and trust anyone ever again.

"It's lucky you got a job here, then," he said finally, gazing down at his cup. "I wish I'd known about her. I wish I'd gotten to meet her."

"You'd have liked her." Luke's voice was soft. "She'd have liked you, too, I think."

"Really?" Stone lifted a brow, but he couldn't deny that the thought of his aunt actually liking him was rather nice. "Not many people like me."

Luke seemed surprised by that. "I don't see why not. Sure, you're on the quiet side, but you ain't the unfriendly kind. Priss weren't overly talkative herself. Sarah was the one who always had a word and a smile for everyone, whether she knew them or not."

Stone shrugged. "I ain't exactly comfortable with most folks. I'm better with animals."

"Nothin' wrong with that." Luke smiled reassuringly. "It don't mean you ain't likable." He paused, fixing Stone with an oddly intense look. "I like you."

Stone felt himself blushing, which he hated. He couldn't help it, though, not when the look in Luke's eyes was so unsettling, making him feel as though Luke could see all his secrets. "I bet you like everyone," he said dryly. "You're just sociable."

Luke laughed and shook his head. "Nah, I don't like everyone, but I've been called a sociable man before. No harm in bein' friendly, after all. Especially to folks who don't like me. Nothin' makes them madder."

That made Stone chuckle, surprising even him. "I can imagine." He finished off his coffee, then rose with a sigh. "I suppose we should get goin'. I'll clean up if you'll hitch up the buggy."

"Sure thing, boss." Luke drained his cup, and then he pushed back his chair and stood up. "I'll see you out front."

Stone nodded and set about clearing the table and washing up. When he finished, he dried his hands, picked up his hat, and headed out the front door, finding that Luke was already there, the buggy hitched to a matched pair of lovely Palominos, their golden hides gleaming in the sunlight. He walked down the steps and stopped for a moment to pat the horses, then pulled himself up into the seat beside Luke. "Ready?"

"I'm ready if you are, boss," Luke replied, nodding at him and giving him a smile that somehow seemed more than just friendly.

Stone looked away, feeling confused again. He was going to either have to get used to Luke and his ways or learn how to run the ranch on his own; neither option set well with him, and he growled silently to himself, crossing his arms over his chest as Luke steered the horses toward the road leading to town.

Luke either didn't notice Stone's crankiness or he wasn't letting it bother him, because he leaned back and hummed "Buffalo Gals" quietly as they rode along. It wasn't until they were almost to town that he spoke again, glancing over at Stone with a mischievous look.

"I reckon you're goin' to have to be a little sociable today. But don't worry. I'll introduce you around, and you can say howdy and leave the rest of the talkin' to me, if you like."

"That's fine," Stone replied, and then sighed. "I suppose I'm goin' to have to make the effort."

"It's natural curiosity." Luke gave him a sympathetic look. "It'll wear off in time. It's just excitin' right now. We don't get many new folks out here."

"Really?" Stone was surprised. "But it's beautiful! I'd think people would be comin' along all the time." He had to admit, if only to himself, he was growing more attached to the ranch every day. "Well, I'll try my best. Sometimes I just don't know what to say."

"Then stick to the basics," Luke suggested. "Say howdy, ask 'em how they are, and say 'that's good to hear' or 'I'm sorry to hear it,' dependin' on what they say back. Most folks will start jawin' at you on their own after that, and all you got to do is listen and nod like it's the most fascinatin' thing in the world. When you get tired of listenin', you say, 'Well, it was nice seein' you,' and that's all there is to it."

Stone's mouth dropped open, and he shut it with a snap. "It can't be that easy, can it?" he asked, shaking his head. He'd spent years fumbling around, looking for words, or, more often, looking to escape. Then Luke came up with a solution like it was the easiest thing in the world. "I'll be damned."

Luke grinned. "It ain't about the talkin', it's about the listenin', and you're good at that. Most folks are happy to talk your ear off, and if you run up on another quiet one, well, you can both be quiet after you get through the 'how are yous', and I reckon you'll both be relieved the socializin' is over."

"Ain't that the truth," Stone muttered. Then he was distracted as the first of the buildings came into sight, indicating they'd reached Serenity.

The town was decent sized, though not as big as a city like Reno or Abilene. Luke had told him there were nearly five hundred people, not counting the hands on the ranches who came into town looking for entertainment. There were two general stores, three banks, several small shops, a schoolhouse, and at least four saloons. Stone frowned at the sight of those, but turned his attention to the big white building coming up on their right, its tall steeple setting it apart from the shorter buildings nearby. Buggies and wagons were pulling up around it, and Stone swallowed hard at the sight of all the people.

"Just smile and say howdy," Luke murmured, clapping him briefly on the shoulder before guiding the horses to a free space at a hitching post. "They're goin' to gawk, but you just let 'em. It won't hurt nothin'. They want to see the new owner of Copper Lake Ranch, that's all."

"It was easier bein' a cowboy," Stone replied grimly. He could feel the weight of eyes on him, and he tilted his chin up. If they were going to look, there wasn't a thing he could do about it. But he'd not hang his head; when the nasty, cutting comments about his parentage came, he'd ignore them as he always had.

He got out of the buggy, straightened his coat, and resisted the urge to fiddle with his tie while he waited for Luke to tie up the horses. Then he moved to Luke's side, doing his best not to frown as they approached the steps of the church and the large knot of people milling around inside.

"Stick close," Luke murmured, and then he began navigating the crowd, tipping his hat and smiling as he greeted the townspeople he knew.

Somehow, he managed to introduce Stone and keep them both moving toward the door at a steady pace, deftly avoiding any clutching hands or nosy questions that would have dragged them into conversation. It seemed like no time at all before Luke was steering him toward a pew near the front, and Stone had just enough time to notice the little brass plaque on the side that read "In loving memory of Daniel Rivers" before they sat down.

"That wasn't so bad, now was it?" Luke gave Stone a beatific smile, offering no clues as to how he'd worked that particular bit of magic.

Stone forced himself to relax against the wooden pew, easing the tension knotted in his shoulders, and looked at Luke gratefully. "I suppose not. You're goin' to have to teach me that trick, though. Seems like it would come in handy."

Luke's smile turned mischievous. "If I teach you all my tricks, you might not have any reason to keep me around, and I'm of a mind to stay."

There was the teasing again, and Stone shook his head, giving a long-suffering sigh. He didn't respond as tartly as he might have, however, given he was sure there were judgmental eyes watching his every move.

"Minds can change," he replied, focusing his attention on the pulpit as the rest of the congregation filed in and took their seats.

"So they can," Luke agreed amiably. "But mine tends to stay made up when I know what I want." He glanced sidelong at Stone with an enigmatic smile. "Just so you know."

A part of Stone wanted to ask what Luke meant by that, but this certainly wasn't the time. Especially since the choir was rising to their feet, and he stood along with everyone else as a piano began to play the opening hymn.

As church services went, Stone decided Reverend Cole's was about middle of the road. He wasn't a fire-and-brimstone type of man, but he wasn't a complete mouse, either. Instead he exhorted his congregation to hard work, soberness, and charity, and managed to wrap up his preaching about five minutes after Stone was beginning to wonder how much longer he'd be able to keep his eyes open.

Then it was time to try to get out of the church, so he pasted a smile on his lips, murmured politely in response to the comments directed at him, and made for the door as quickly as humanly possible, hoping Luke could work his magic if Stone got bogged down. Fortunately, it seemed most people were as anxious to escape as he was, probably looking forward to getting home to Sunday dinner and a little relaxation before the week started up again.

He made it to the door, shook hands with the preacher, clapped his hat on his head, and started down the steps, counting himself lucky for having escaped cleanly. Unfortunately, that was when his luck ran out.

"Mr. Harrison!" Stone turned at the sound of his name and fought the urge to beat a hasty retreat as he saw a large, determined matron step out from around the bush she must have been hiding behind. She was smiling widely at him, and Stone was oddly reminded of a big dog that looked friendly until just before it bit you.

"Ma'am," Stone said, glancing around for Luke without being too obvious about it, but he didn't seem to be around just when Stone needed him the most.

"Lovely to meet you," the matron said, holding out a plump hand for Stone to take. "I'm Mrs. James Wilson. My husband is the doctor here in town. Your dear aunt was such a good friend of mine. We were almost like sisters."

Stone took her hand, shaking it briefly. "Pleased to meet you." He didn't know what else to say, seeing as he hadn't known his aunt at all.

"I know it must be hard, you being new in town and all," Mrs. Wilson continued, apparently unperturbed by Stone's terse greeting. "I'd be remiss in not inviting you to Sunday dinner with my family. Dear Priscilla would probably haunt me! And you wouldn't have to worry about being with a couple of stuffy old people, either. My daughter Agnes still lives at home, and I know she'd be delighted if you'd join us."

Stone's eyes widened in horror at the thought of having to take a meal with complete strangers and try to make small talk as they'd no doubt expect him to do. Mrs. Wilson seemed the type to try to worm his whole life story out of him, and he could only imagine how well tales of his drunk father would go over.

Fortunately, Luke appeared at his side and spoke up before he had to. "I'm so sorry, Mrs. Wilson." Luke gave the formidable matron an apologetic smile. "I'm sure Mr. Harrison would love to have dinner with you and your family, but I already made him promise to go over the books with me right after church. I've been awful hard on him, I know, deprivin' him of such good food and good company, but I'm tryin' to do right by the ranch." He captured her hand and kissed the back of it, flashing a winning smile at her. "You understand, I'm sure."

"Well, I can hardly drag a man away from business when he's just getting settled in." Stone watched in amazement as Mrs. Wilson, who had to be in her late fifties, simpered at Luke and actually batted her eyelashes at him like she was some coy miss in her teens. "And we all know how well you took care of dear Priscilla and watched over the ranch. Perhaps another time, then?" She looked at Stone. "Next Sunday?"

Eyes wide, Stone looked at Luke. If the man could rescue him from this one, he'd owe him in a big way.

Luke gave her dimpled hand a squeeze, and his smile turned beguiling. "I'm awful sorry, ma'am, but I'm goin' to be keepin' Mr. Harrison right busy for a while to come. He's never run a ranch before, and I want to teach him right. It's what Mrs. Harrison would have wanted," he added with a hint of piety. "How about if Mr. Harrison lets you know when I've finally freed him from his shackles?"

"Oh." Mrs. Wilson looked disappointed, but Luke's charm seemed to take the wind out of her sails. "Of course. I understand. Please do let me know, Mr. Harrison. We'd love to have you any time."

"Thank you, ma'am," Stone replied. He darted a glance at Luke to make sure that was a good enough response.

"Afternoon, ma'am." Luke tipped his hat and gave her one last smile before he subtly steered Stone away. "Give Miss Agnes my regards."

"I will," she replied. Stone waited until they'd gotten around to the side of the church, then let out a huge sigh of relief.

"I thought I was doomed," he whispered, glancing around to make sure no more dowagers were going to spring out of the bushes. "Thanks."

Luke chuckled quietly, his eyes alight with amusement. "Any time, boss. I shoulda warned you, but I didn't think about it. Miss Agnes has the face of a horse and the figure of a pine post, and Mrs. Wilson's been tryin' to marry her off to anything in long pants for years, but no one'll take her. Pity, because she's a real nice girl and smart as a whip. I'd snap her up in a minute if I was the marryin' kind."

Stone couldn't help shivering in horror at the thought. Not that he cared what the poor girl looked like, but if Mrs. Wilson was angling to catch him for her daughter within an hour of him coming to town for the first time, how many other women were going to be following behind?

He realized he was considered an attractive man, and more than one woman had made her interest in him obvious over the years. Mostly he avoided the issue entirely by ignoring it, and fortunately no woman had considered a transient cowboy who obviously didn't have much money to be worth pursuing too hard. But now he was the owner of a large, prosperous ranch, and if he was going to make a go of things, it was important to keep the good will of the townsfolk. Not to mention, he didn't want to give any of them cause to go looking so close at him they figured out things he'd rather they didn't know.

"Well, I do appreciate it." He gave Luke a lopsided smile. "I guess we should get back to the ranch before we're ambushed again. I'd thought to offer to buy you dinner here in town to show how much I appreciate your help, but maybe that wouldn't be such a good idea."

"Probably not," Luke agreed. "Word gets around pretty quick, and Mrs. Wilson wouldn't be too happy with either of us. You'd probably get roped into dinner next Sunday."

Stone nodded and headed toward the buggy. "I heat up a mean can of beans," he said, his expression deadpan. "Will that do instead?"

"I'm happy to take whatever you want to give me," Luke replied, keeping pace with him easily.

Stone felt his face growing hot, and shot Luke an aggrieved look. The man was doing it again, saying things Stone didn't know how to take. But unlike Mrs. Wilson, at least Stone was sure Luke didn't mean him any harm. He didn't know why he was coming to trust the man easier than he could remember trusting anyone in a long time, especially given how Luke confused him, but his gut was telling him Luke Reynolds was a good man, and Stone had learned to trust his instincts on such things a very long time ago.

He gave Luke a smile that an angel couldn't have done better. "I'll remember that when it's time to discuss your salary."

Luke laughed outright at that and raised one eyebrow at him, looking like the devil to Stone's angel. "Does that mean I can take it in trade?"

"Sure." Stone decided he wasn't going to look at that comment too closely. "You can have all the cattle you can carry."

"That's mighty generous of you, boss," Luke replied, still grinning. "Maybe we can negotiate after a month or two. I wouldn't mind workin' my way up from cattle."

"Well, I hope to be considered a reasonable boss, so I'm willin' to listen." They reached the buggy, and Stone untied the reins from the post and tossed them to Luke. "Come on, let's get home. I've had enough of town to last me quite a while."

Luke caught the reins neatly and took his place in the driver's seat, and as soon as Stone was settled beside him, he set the team in motion. "Home it is, boss, and maybe we can find something a little more tasty than a can of beans in the larder."

"Maybe we can," Stone replied, and then settled back with a quiet sigh of contentment. Although he'd never admit it, he'd rather have cold beans in Luke's company than be served the finest, fanciest food in the world by someone like Mrs. Wilson. Luke might confuse him from time to time, but at least he wasn't expecting Stone to be someone he couldn't be. Simple acceptance was a gift that cost nothing, but to Stone, it was more rare and precious than gold.

6

STEPHEN'S Mercantile on Serenity's Main Street wasn't large, but it had everything a rancher needed. It had never occurred to Stone just how many cans of beans and sacks of flour it took to keep hungry ranch hands fed, although he didn't begrudge them any of it. Every hand on the Copper Lake worked hard, and Stone knew good, hot meals every day helped keep them going.

The ranch had a standing order for the main supplies, which were brought in by train to Reno and shipped by wagon to Serenity and other small towns between the big spreads. There was some local farming, and Mary helped keep up a garden at Copper Lake that Sarah had planted years before, which gave them things like tomatoes and greens, but this late in October, everything had been harvested, so any extras had to be purchased. As Stone picked up the items on Mary's list, along with a few things for himself, he brought them back to the counter, where Mr. Stephens, the owner of the store, totted up the bill.

Stone had been at the ranch for almost a month now, and things were really starting to make sense to him. He might lack a bit on book learning, but he could balance ledgers and write letters just fine, especially with Luke's help.

The thought of Luke made Stone frown, but not because the man had done anything wrong. On the contrary, Luke was the very model of a perfect ranch foreman; he could do anything the hands could do, and he could give the men orders and they'd listen to him. He could charm even the most sullen cowboy into smiling, and where Stone might have been tempted to get angry, Luke was patient and humorous, and it had a much better effect on the men.

The problem was that Luke made Stone feel things he had no business feeling.

It was hard enough being a quarter Pawnee in a white man's world, but being a man who didn't care for women, well, that was a crime in most folks' books. He couldn't let it get out of hand, because they both had too much to lose.

As Stone turned down one aisle, he stopped suddenly, having almost run into a tall, thin woman with mousy brown hair. She was dressed well, but nothing could hide that she wasn't padded the way most men preferred women to be, and her face was plain and freckled. Yet she smiled at him with sweetness, and Stone nodded to her, recognizing Mrs. Wilson's daughter, Agnes.

"Morning, ma'am," he greeted her, hoping she wasn't about to gush an invitation to dinner at him the way her mother had. So far, Luke had managed to keep all the matrons and their daughters at bay, but he was outside getting the supplies loaded in the wagon, and Stone was on his own.

"Good morning." Agnes held out her hand, her gaze direct and friendly, without any of the coy simpering he'd seen from some of the local gals. He took her hand, and her grip was firm and surprisingly solid. "You're Mr. Harrison, of course. And no doubt you know I'm Agnes Wilson."

"Yes, ma'am." Stone released her hand and fumbled for something to say. "Luke pointed you out to me at church."

Agnes nodded. "I do hope Mama has stopped pestering you about dinner." Her smile became slightly crooked. "She's a darling, really, but she just won't give up until she finds me a husband, whether he wants to be found or not. I'm sorry if she's bothered you."

The directness surprised Stone, but he was comfortable with people who didn't play games with words, and he found himself comfortable with her. "Well, Miss Agnes, a lot of the mamas in town seem to be of the same mind, so you don't need to apologize."

That made her chuckle, her brown eyes dancing in genuine amusement. "I hope they haven't overwhelmed you. You're a ranch owner, and that makes you a prime target. Just hold your ground unless you find a girl you really do like. If you give an inch, you'll probably find yourself standing in front of the preacher before you know what happened." She lowered her voice and leaned closer. "To be honest, I've seen more than one groom at the altar on his wedding day looking a little confused about how he got there."

Despite his innate reserve, Stone grinned. "Serenity ain't the only place it happens," he confided. "I reckon mamas are the same all over."

"I reckon they are."

Luke strolled up to the two of them, regarding them curiously. "Mornin', Miss Agnes," he added, touching his hat politely. "I beg your pardon for interruptin', but we got the wagon loaded up, and I came to see if Mr. Harrison needed an extra hand."

Stone looked at Luke, unable to help noticing the curve of his lips as he smiled at Agnes Wilson. "I'm about done." He tore his gaze away, looking back to Agnes. "Miss Agnes and I were just havin' a little talk."

"Good morning, Luke." Agnes smiled in a friendly fashion. "I hope you're doing well."

"Can't complain much, although my new boss here does run me ragged," Luke teased, and as he turned to look at Stone, the polite friendliness he showed to Agnes deepened into warmth, and his smile widened.

Stone felt his face heating up, as it usually did when Luke teased him in front of other people, and his reply was gruff. "Only because I have to keep you busy and out of mischief."

Agnes glanced between the two of them, one eyebrow raised in surprise, but then she smiled. "He's got you there, Luke," she said primly. "Which shows Mr. Harrison is a very insightful man."

Luke laughed, obviously not taking any offense to his teasing being turned back on him. "That he is," he agreed, eyes alight with amusement. "He may not say much, but he don't miss nothin'."

"I can see that." Agnes nodded to them. "Well, I won't keep you, gentlemen. I know you must be anxious to get back to the ranch." She rested her hand on Stone's arm. "And don't worry, Mr. Harrison. Mama won't be bothering you about dinner again. I'll make certain of it."

Stone was surprised, but he wasn't about to look at a gift horse in the mouth. "Why, thank you, Miss Agnes. I—um—I mean—"

Agnes shook her head and patted his arm before stepping back. "Oh you haven't hurt my feelings, Mr. Harrison. As it so happens, I'm not looking to get married, at least not right now. I suspect I'll know the right man when I see him, if I ever do. No amount of wishing and hoping by my mama is going to make you interested in me anyway, and I'd rather have you as a friend, like Luke, than dreading the sight of me. Now then, I'll see you gentlemen on Sunday at church."

With another sweet smile at them, she gathered her skirts and turned away. Stone looked after her in surprise, and then he turned to Luke. "That's one smart lady."

Luke watched her go, his expression speculative. "That she is," he agreed, glancing at Stone. "Some man's goin' to be right lucky to have her one day."

Stone nodded. If he *had* been interested in women, Agnes Wilson would have been at the top of his list, no matter what she looked like. There was something wrong with the men in this town if they couldn't recognize what a catch she was. "Guess we'd better get back to the ranch. Still a lot to do before the snow flies."

They headed toward the counter, and Stone had the feeling he'd somehow managed to make a friend in Agnes.

42

7

LUKE was tired after a long day in the saddle, but it was a good sort of tired, one he welcomed as a respite from all the necessary bookwork he and Stone had been poring over of late. They were on the back end of November, which meant the grazing season was over, and the ranch wouldn't have a steady income for a few months, not even from the copper mine. The bank account was padded comfortably enough they wouldn't have to quibble over pennies, but Luke was thrifty, and he never liked seeing more money going out than was coming in. He'd be a lot happier when spring rolled around and they would sell cattle and horses at the market and begin working in the mine again.

Stone didn't seem happy about it either, but Luke explained winter was a time to hunker down, trying to reassure himself as much as Stone. It was a time to make sure the fences held, and the livestock survived, and not much else. It was too cold and dangerous to send anyone into the mines, and riding the fence was more dangerous at this time of year than any other, considering how a storm could blow in and take a man unawares.

Today, however, they'd put the ledgers aside and ridden out to check the fence near the lake. It had been repaired over the summer, and Luke wanted to make sure it was holding up. If there were repairs to be made or patching to be done, he wanted it done sooner rather than later to prepare for the long, cold months ahead.

Together, he and Stone had covered more ground than he thought they would, which pleased him. They made a good team, he thought as he glanced over at Stone, who was working in silence, as usual. If he'd learned anything over the last few weeks, it was that the two of them definitely weren't two peas in a pod. To his mind, they were more like salt and pepper: different flavors, but both necessary to make a good meal. And he thought they would be spicy as hell in bed, but so far, it was wishful thinking on his part.

He grabbed a hoof pick and lifted Mist's left foreleg, focusing on cleaning her hoof before he got caught staring at Stone like a calf-eyed idiot. He'd been teasing and flirting a little, trying to show Stone how interested he was without pushing too hard, but either Stone didn't see it or he didn't *want* to see it. Sometimes, Luke thought he saw a glimmer of awareness in those dark eyes, but it never went anywhere, and Luke had been a lot friendlier with his right hand lately thanks to Stone Harrison.

Sometimes, he wondered if it would be worth the risk to grab Stone, kiss him, and see if maybe *that* got the message across loud and clear since being subtle hadn't worked worth a damn, but as skittish as Stone was, he'd probably bolt. No, Luke would have to be patient and wear him down until he was ready to see how good it could be between them. Until then, Luke saw a lot more buckets of ice-cold well water in his future.

"Doin' all right, boss?" He knew if there was going to be any talk between them, he'd have to start it. "I didn't work you too hard today, did I?" he added with a grin to show he was teasing.

"That'll be the day," Stone replied mildly. He was brushing Raider's coat, taking his time about it as though he really enjoyed the task. "I've ridden more miles of fence than I care to think about, and most of it was in far worse shape." He looked over his shoulder at Luke. "You do a good job keepin' things fixed up. I bet my aunt would be pleased."

Luke paused to watch Stone run the brush along Raider's side and follow it with his hand, his long fingers caressing the horse with obvious affection, and Luke tried hard not to feel jealous of a damned *horse*. But if Stone liked touching enough to enjoy brushing a horse that much, Luke could only imagine what he'd be like with another person.

"I hope she would," he replied at last. "But Copper Lake is my home, too, and I take pride in what's mine. My name ain't on the deed, but as long as I'm foreman here, I've got a reputation to uphold."

"True." Stone stopped brushing Raider, turning around to face Luke, his expression pensive. "I sure couldn't run this place without you. I just hope I'm pullin' my weight."

"You're doin' fine." Luke lowered Mist's foreleg carefully. "Especially for someone who didn't know beans about running a ranch a couple of months ago. You can't expect to learn it all in a few weeks."

Stone shrugged, but his lips quirked up in a tiny smile Luke had come to recognize meant he was pleased. "I'm tryin'. Guess I never thought I'd ever be nothin' but a cowboy."

Luke thought Stone had probably been more than just a cowboy even when he was a cowboy. Though Stone had been tight-lipped about his past, Luke had picked up on enough to understand Stone hadn't had an easy time of it. He was a smart, hard-working man who'd never had the chance to show what he was capable of, but Copper Lake was changing all that, and Luke aimed to help him use the untapped potential he'd been carrying around.

"Well, I guess you were wrong about that," Luke replied. "But you'll do all right. You ain't afraid of gettin' your hands dirty, and that's good. Too many men would feel like they'd been dropped into the lap of luxury, but runnin' a place like this takes hard work from everybody, not just the hands."

That earned him a smile. "Wouldn't know what to do with luxury anyway." Stone put the brush back on its shelf, picked up a cloth and a bottle of oil, and set about working on his saddle. "Seems it might be dull. Not enough to do."

"Oh I don't know," Luke drawled, deciding he'd gone long enough without teasing Stone a little bit. He enjoyed seeing Stone blush; he'd never seen anything more becoming on a man or woman in his life, and it made him want to nuzzle Stone's rosy cheeks. "I can think of a few leisure-time activities that wouldn't be dull at all. Well, if they're done right, that is."

Stone looked up, and Luke saw the desired flush rising on his cheeks and the confusion in his eyes. It was as if Stone thought Luke *might* be hinting at what he actually was, but Stone was either unwilling or afraid to believe it. Or maybe he was afraid to act on it, since he'd been careful not to admit openly his preferences were just like Luke's.

Finally, Stone made a noncommittal sound and reached for the bottle of Neatsfoot oil, but in an uncharacteristically clumsy move, he knocked it over, splattering it all over the arm and chest of his blue shirt.

"Damn," he muttered in annoyance as he mopped up the spillage with the cloth he'd been using on his saddle. He put the cork back in the bottle and began to unbutton his shirt. "Mary's goin' to kill me."

And you're goin' to kill me, Luke thought dazedly as he followed the path of Stone's fingers down the front of his shirt, watching eagerly for a hint of bare skin.

"Yeah, that one might have to go straight to the rag bag." Luke had to force the words past the dryness in his throat. "If the weather's clear, you can go into town and buy a new shirt tomorrow, though."

Stone slipped the shirt off his shoulders. Luke saw Stone's torso was almost as dark as his forearms, and he had very little body hair anywhere in sight. His shoulders were broad, and he had a few scars that stood out prominently, lighter in hue than his skin.

"Maybe I can get it out," he said, fetching a bucket of water from the trough. He picked up the saddle soap and dipped it in the bucket along with his shirt. "Hate to waste a good shirt."

"I think there's an old washboard the hands use around here somewhere." Luke had to tear his gaze away from the sight of Stone's muscles working beneath his smooth skin. There wasn't any sense in torturing himself by looking at what he couldn't touch, he reminded himself sternly as he went to find the washboard and brought it back to Stone. "Here, maybe this'll help."

"Thanks." Stone had put the bucket on the workbench, and as he reached out to take the washboard, their eyes met. Stone went still, staring at him as though he was reading something on Luke's face, and for the first time, the awareness in Stone's eyes was more than just a faint spark. There was no mistaking the sudden flare of heat in that dark gaze or the way Stone's breathing suddenly sped up.

Luke wasn't sure he could look away even if he'd wanted to, but he didn't; he was losing himself in the depths of Stone's eyes, captive and captivated all at once, and he didn't want to be set free. *Oh Lord,* he thought with a silent groan, *I've gone and fallen for him!* It was quite possibly the most stupid thing he'd ever done, but it was too late now. He was well and truly hooked, and he had no choice but to keep on trying to hook Stone in return.

"Any time, boss." He licked his dry lips as he released the washboard, but not Stone's gaze. Whatever Stone was seeing in his face, well, it was too late to hide it now, and he didn't care to try.

There was a flicker in Stone's eyes, and then Stone took a step toward him, close enough that Luke could feel the warmth radiating from his skin. Stone moved like a wolf stalking his prey, and he lifted his hand and reached out as though he might be about to touch Luke's face.

The moment was shattered by a sound at the stable door at the far end, a laugh and the dull thud of hooves as some of the hands returned from their chores. A shutter slammed down over Stone's face, and he abruptly turned away, plunging the washboard into the bucket and scrubbing at his shirt with unusual vigor.

"Damn it," Luke muttered as he, too, turned away and suppressed the urge to shoot dire glares at the hands who had destroyed the first promising sign Stone was responding to him.

It wasn't their fault; it was just bad timing, and Luke released a quiet sigh, glancing wistfully at Stone, who seemed intent on ignoring his presence entirely, as if to make up for the momentary lapse. They had a long winter ahead of them and plenty of nights alone in the big house. Luke would be patient and wait, and the next time, he'd make damned sure there wouldn't be any hands barging in to interrupt.

8

STONE stepped out the kitchen door, his gaze moving to the sky as he scanned the pale gray expanse. He didn't like the look of it or the way the wind was kicking up out of the west. Not at all. They'd had a few light snowfalls in the last three weeks, but nothing had stuck around for more than a couple of days. The hands were glad, since the mild, dry weather made their jobs a lot easier.

He pulled his collar up around his ears to block the breeze and headed toward the wood pile to fetch more for the fireplace. The temperature was dropping slowly, not quite at freezing though the wind made it feel a lot colder. No one seemed too concerned except for Stone. Something about the way the wind smelled warned him a bad blow might be coming.

"Don't be stupid," he muttered. He'd spent most of his life farther south and not so near the mountains, so he wasn't used to the vagaries of the weather in these parts. But he remembered his mother teaching him you could tell when a storm was coming by the way the air smelled: the sharp tang of a thunderstorm or the dry, almost dusty smell of a blizzard. He looked back over his shoulder at the mountains, looming clear and close under the cloud cover. There was snow on their slopes, but not much, and mostly in the shady spots where the sun couldn't reach. The mountains didn't look worried, so he told himself to forget the way his nose itched and get on with the chores. He had enough to do with Luke out taking care of a break in the fence where a big tree had fallen on the far side of the lake and taken down a large section of wire.

By rights, Stone should be out there helping, but he'd started going out with different hands on his rounds of riding fence, telling Luke he needed to get to know the other men better. Luke had given him a wry glance but hadn't protested, although Stone suspected Luke knew exactly why he was doing it. It was why Stone had told Luke he could handle the books on his own now and why he'd started going up to bed earlier in the evenings; Stone was afraid of what might happen if he was alone with Luke too long.

He'd tried to deny it, telling himself Luke was trying to get a rise out of him; just because Luke had admitted he preferred male company didn't necessarily mean he was looking at *Stone* that way. Nor did Stone want him to. Some things were dangerous and best left alone, and Stone had long ago learned he could ignore his physical needs if he tried hard enough. And *damn*, he'd been trying hard ever since that day in the stable when Luke had turned around and looked at him like he'd wanted to devour Stone whole right then and there.

That look had told Stone he'd been fooling himself. Luke wanted him, and he'd felt his own desire rising to meet Luke's with sudden, almost overwhelming power. No one had ever made him feel like he could lose control and not care about the consequences. Not even Daniel, the first man he'd been with.

He hadn't thought about Daniel in almost a decade, and he didn't want to think about him now, but it seemed inevitable that his desire for Luke would stir up those long-denied memories. Daniel had been nearly thirty, and Stone had been only eighteen and vulnerable after the death of his mother. Daniel was the owner of a saloon in Moapa, and he'd rented an upstairs room to Stone and his mother during the last year of her life. Daniel had been kind, and somehow after the funeral, Stone had ended up drunk and miserable at the door to Daniel's room, which had been right down the hall from his. He couldn't bear to sleep in that room and not hear the quiet sound of his mother breathing, and Daniel had opened his door, letting Stone in without question and then taking him to bed and showing him life went on. He'd not even minded when Stone had wept for his mother afterward.

Daniel had let him stay and had never pushed Stone to sleep with him, but Stone did anyway. It wasn't love, but gratitude; Stone knew that, because if he'd loved Daniel, maybe he wouldn't have felt so afraid and ashamed. But the physical pleasure gave Stone a respite from the aching pain and loneliness of knowing that all the family he cared about was gone, and for that, he knew he'd never be able to repay what Daniel had done for him.

It wasn't meant to last, and Stone figured out he needed to be somewhere else when whispers started up about Daniel and his "Injun boy." He'd told Daniel he was leaving, and while Daniel hadn't tried to talk him out of it, he'd given Stone enough money to buy a horse and a saddle. Stone had bought Raider, turned eastward, and never looked back.

He wondered at times how Daniel had known what Stone was, if there was something he'd given away that indicated he was far more interested in the men who came into the saloon than the women who danced there. He was well aware that the direction of his interest, especially combined with his mixed blood, was something that could get him killed, and so he'd tried not to think about anyone that way, male or female. He'd slipped a couple of times, when he'd been foolish enough to let himself get near a bottle of whiskey, and he'd ended up in some dark room fumbling around with someone he barely knew just to ease the ache of loneliness. But that hadn't happened in a long time, not since the last time he'd had a drink, nearly seven years ago, and had ended up with a bullet through his shoulder when the cowboy he'd thought was interested in him turned out to be anything but.

But the situation with Luke was different, just as Stone was a different man, no longer the innocent boy who'd gone knocking on Daniel's door. For the first time, he had a place to call his own, a chance to build a life that wasn't based on working for someone else. To be his own man, to steer the course of his life. This ranch had come to mean more to him than anything else in the two short months he'd been here. He felt a connection to the land, pride and joy in the beauty of it, and he knew he'd protect it with everything he had. This was now his *home*, and there wasn't any place else he'd rather be.

Part of what made up that feeling, though, was one smart-mouthed, grinning cowboy with a gleam in his eye and a teasing word on his lips. A cowboy who seemed quite willing to take Stone as he was and even take him to bed. And that was the one thing Stone knew could never happen.

People talked. He knew it, and Luke sure knew it, since he'd played the role of chaperone for Priss and her Sarah. They'd had to hide things so folks wouldn't get the wrong idea and come after them. There were a lot of people in the world who were filled with hate for anything and anyone different, and Stone had run afoul of that attitude far more often than he liked. But being part Pawnee would pale in comparison to the condemnation he'd face for doing what he wanted to do with Luke.

No matter what his body was saying, he couldn't act on it. It would cost too much for him and Luke both, especially for something that could end so badly in other ways. Stone might have been willing to walk away from Daniel, but he had the feeling he wouldn't be able to walk away from Luke—and it just might kill him if Luke was the one who decided to do the walking.

A sudden gust of wind almost blew Stone's hat off and snapped him out of his reverie. He filled his arms with wood and turned back to the house, and then he stopped and stared at the sight before him. Thick, roiling clouds were pouring over the mountain, and beneath them, the rocks that had been bare only minutes before were completely invisible beneath a blanket of snow.

"Blizzard," he muttered, dropping the wood and running toward the bunkhouse. The wind was suddenly roaring around his ears, and as he opened the door, a strong gust made it crash against the wall. He didn't really need to say much; the hands could feel the wind, and flakes of snow blew into the room.

"Are all the cattle in the lower pasture?"

"Yeah, we got back less than half an hour ago from movin' them," a hand named Mason replied as he tugged on his coat. "But some of the horses are in the field out near the road to town. We'd best bring them back to the stable."

"Right." Stone nodded and looked around with a frown, counting heads. "Who went with Luke to work on the fence?"

There was silence for a few moments, and then an older hand whom everyone called Shorty—because he was the tallest of them— spoke up. "I was with him, but he sent me back a while ago. Said he could finish up himself."

Stone felt his stomach drop to the floor. Luke was at the opposite side of the lake and probably not dressed nearly well enough for a blizzard. As fast as the storm was moving in, he was going to get caught in it unless he'd started back at least half an hour ago. It looked to be a whiteout, and that could kill even the most experienced cowboy.

"You get the horses. I'll get Luke." He didn't wait for a reply before hurrying back to the house to grab his extra coat and a scarf, donning the second coat over the one he was wearing and using the scarf to tie his hat on his head. Then he was out the door again.

He ran for the stable, tacking up Raider as quickly as he could, and he tied extra blankets to the back of the saddle. Then he mounted and spurred Raider into a gallop, praying he wasn't too late as he rode into the oncoming storm.

One thing that had served Stone well in his life was a natural born sense of direction. He seemed to always know which way he was going, and he never got lost. When he was a child, his mother had said it was because he came from a long line of trackers whose survival depended on being able to get where they needed to go, no matter what. The ability had always been a part of him, and he hoped it didn't fail him now as the world blurred into a hell of frozen white and whipping wind.

He leaned down low over Raider's neck, guiding the horse with his knees as he peered ahead. The wind was pushing against him and

Raider, trying to drive them back, but he pressed on, hoping to meet Luke quickly.

The snow was coming down sideways and piling up fast. In what seemed like no time, Raider was slogging through drifts higher than his knees, but Stone still urged him forward. It was close to a mile and a half from the ranch house to where Luke would have been working, and Stone knew he wasn't even halfway there.

A few minutes later, however, he saw a dark form against the white, moving erratically off to the south, obviously following the direction of the wind. He altered course toward it, and to his relief, he recognized Mist, her head bent as she pushed through the deepening drifts. He could see Luke's dark form hunkered down over her back.

"Luke! This way!" he yelled, but his voice was whipped away by the wind. He finally caught up with Mist and reached out to shake Luke's shoulder. "Hey! Luke! You're goin' the wrong way!"

Luke jerked as if he'd been startled out of a dream, and he peered at Stone blearily. "Wrong way?"

Now that he was close, Stone could see Luke was shivering, and his skin was already pale from the cold.

"Well, damn." Luke wavered in the saddle and then slumped forward again, closing his eyes. "I just want to sleep…."

"No, you can't sleep yet," Stone shouted. This wouldn't do; if Luke fell unconscious, he could die. Stone wavered for a moment, and then he came to a decision. It would put a lot of strain on Raider, but he thought the big horse could handle it better than Mist could.

He turned Raider around so he and Mist were facing away from the wind, and then he bent and pulled Luke's left foot out of his stirrup. "You've got to help me, cowboy. Come on now. We have to get you home."

Luke responded weakly, but he managed to help enough that Stone was able to get his left leg lifted over Raider's saddle, and then Stone steeled himself and used all his strength to heave Luke off Mist and onto Raider. "Sorry," he murmured, knowing Luke would probably have bruises later, but it was better than dying from exposure. He settled Luke's back against his chest and twisted to untie the blankets from Raider's saddle. It was difficult, but at last, he managed to retrieve them, and he wrapped them around himself and draped them across Luke, shielding him as much as he could from the wind and hoping his body heat would be enough to keep Luke warm. Then he tied Mist's reins to Raider's saddle, wrapped his arms around Luke's waist, and started Raider toward home.

"Talk to me, Luke," he muttered, his lips close to Luke's ear. "Come on, don't you have nothin' to say? That ain't like you."

"You're warm." Luke leaned heavily against him. "But this ain't how I wanted to get your arms around me."

"You ain't never satisfied, are you?" Stone asked, but there was no heat in his words. He was too relieved Luke was still alive and breathing. "Just keep talking and don't go to sleep. Talk about Priss, or the ranch, or Mist. Whatever pops in that foolish head of yours."

For a moment, it seemed as if Luke had nodded off, but when Stone jostled him a little, he began to talk, rambling from one thing to another, beginning with his first day working for Priss and moving on to tell Stone about how he was there when Mist was born. By the time they made it back to the barn, Stone knew more about Luke than he'd ever thought to know about a single person, but at least he'd kept Luke from falling asleep.

The barn door opened a crack as they rode up, and then it was pushed wide enough for him to ride inside. A couple of the hands were within, tending to the horses they had rounded up from the field.

"Was hopin' you'd make it back, boss." Shorty grinned up at him as he untied Mist's reins. "Luke okay?"

"He's been better," Stone replied. A couple of men helped get Luke out of the saddle, and then Stone dismounted. "Can you take care of the horses? I need to get him into the house and warmed up."

"I'm okay." Luke batted away the men who were helping him stay upright, but when he tried to walk and nearly fell flat on his face, he didn't protest a second time. "'Cept for not bein' able to feel my feet," he added, sounding sheepish.

Shorty shook his head. "When you do start feelin' them, you'll wish you couldn't. Go on, boss. We'll take care of this. You need any help gettin' him to the house?"

"No, I can manage. Thanks." Stone lifted Luke's arm across his shoulders and slid his arm around Luke's waist. "You'll be home in no time, cowboy. Just hang in there a few minutes longer, okay?"

True to his word, he got Luke into the house, sighing with relief as the door slammed closed behind them and the warmth of the kitchen blocked out the wind. He lowered Luke carefully into a chair. Luke was a lot paler than Stone would have liked, and he knew he had to get Luke warmed up quickly.

"I need to get your shoes and gloves off and have a look, all right?"

Luke slumped in the chair, still seeming drowsy, but he wasn't so out of it he couldn't muster up a cheeky response. "You can take off whatever you want, boss. I don't mind you lookin'."

"I'll look, all right. You just better hope I like what I see."

He got Luke's boots and socks off, and then leaned in to peer closely at Luke's toes. They were pale and cold, and Stone removed his gloves and gently touched them, pleased he couldn't see any damage. Then he did the same thing with Luke's hands, finally sighing with relief as he pressed Luke's cold fingers gently between his palms to warm them. "Looks like we won't be callin' you Stumpy, after all. But I need to get you upstairs and out of those wet clothes. You aren't going to want to be on those feet when the feelin' comes back."

Ten minutes later, he had Luke upstairs, undressed, and tucked between the covers of his bed. He went downstairs and rummaged in the cabinet until he found a bottle of whiskey. With a little help from a bleary Luke, he managed to get a good amount of whiskey down Luke's throat. He hoped it would help blur the awful, stinging sensation once feeling started coming back to Luke's numb feet.

Each ranch bedroom had a fireplace, and before long, it was almost too warm. Stone looked closely at Luke, but he seemed to have gone to sleep, and so he shrugged out of his coat, took off his boots, and sat down in the chair by Luke's bed. Stone closed his eyes and rubbed his forehead, and then he started to tremble as his emotions kicked in now that Luke was safe.

Luke had come within minutes of losing his fingers and toes and within maybe a half hour of dying, and it was all because of him. This wouldn't have happened if Stone had been out there with Luke and doing his part. He'd let his fear stand in the way of doing his duty, and Luke had nearly paid a terrible price because of it.

Guilt made Stone want to cringe with shame. Luke was probably going to be angry at him for what had happened, but he couldn't be any angrier than Stone was at himself. It didn't matter that Luke was the foreman and was just doing his job. Stone was the *boss*, and that made him responsible for everyone, even Luke. Perhaps especially Luke.

"I'm sorry," he murmured, opening his eyes and looking at Luke's face, relieved to see his cheeks beginning to lose their pallor. Luke didn't move, and Stone reached out and rested his hand against Luke's cheek. *I'm just checking that he's warming up*, he told himself, though he knew it was a lie. He'd been lying to himself a lot lately, it seemed, about a lot of things, and it made him hurt in a way he'd not felt in a long time.

Luke moved, and Stone snatched his hand back, not wanting Luke to catch him in a moment of weakness. Then his eyes fell on the whiskey bottle, and he shivered. He was cold, too, and not just from the weather. One sip couldn't hurt, right? He was at home, and Luke was sleeping. Just a little sip of whiskey to help dull his pain.

He picked up the bottle, sloshing the liquor into the same glass he'd used for Luke, and then he tilted his head back and downed the alcohol before he could think better of it. It burned all the way down his throat, but it felt good, too. It warmed him, and soon enough, it would blunt the edges of his guilt and help him get through this night so he could face whatever happened tomorrow.

Would Luke be angry enough to leave? Stone stared into the glass and shivered again. He didn't want Luke to leave. He couldn't do anything about the attraction that seemed to be pulling them together, and he didn't want Luke out of his life. But if Luke wanted to leave, what could Stone do to stop him? And Luke had a right to be angry, whether he realized it or not. He poured more whiskey; he wasn't numb enough yet. The second glass burned less, and warmed him more.

"That's all," he said, putting the glass on the table. He looked at Luke again and shifted the chair closer to the bed. He needed to close his eyes for a few minutes, but he wanted to make sure he would hear if Luke woke up. So he lay his head down on the mattress by Luke's shoulder, and as the guilt was dulled by the alcohol, Stone drifted off to sleep.

—— 9 ——

THE feeling of someone stroking his hair roused Stone, and in the twilight state between sleeping and waking, he thought it was his mother, soothing him once more as she had so many times when he was a boy. But then he woke enough to remember she was gone, and he lifted his head to find Luke watching him with what seemed to be affection, not the expected anger and recrimination.

"You could've gotten in here with me," Luke drawled, the teasing gleam appearing in his eyes. "I wouldn't have minded."

Stone relaxed, his worries about everything seeming to fade before the warmth in Luke's eyes. "Yeah?" He gave Luke a lazy smile. Why had he fought the attraction between them? He couldn't remember, and he really didn't care. "And what would you do if I did?"

Luke's smile took on a decidedly wicked tilt. "Whatever I could get away with."

"That sounds like it could be interestin'." Luke was irresistible when he smiled like that, and Stone licked his lips, wondering how that smile would taste. "What would you do first?"

Luke was silent for a moment, a questioning look in his eyes. "You really want to know?"

"Yeah." Stone sat up and stared at Luke challengingly. "What would you do with me, cowboy? If I said you could do anythin' you wanted."

"Oh, that's easy." Luke's voice was low and husky, and Stone saw a heated gleam in his eyes. "I'd want to kiss you first. I've been dyin' to know if you taste as good as you look."

"Have you now?" Stone liked the sound of that. He'd wondered how Luke tasted, too, and now he wanted to find out. He moved closer and shot Luke a challenging look. "Then why don't you get over here and do it?"

A flash of shock crossed Luke's face, and it seemed Stone had managed to shut his mouth, which was definitely a first, but he didn't take long to recover. Shifting to lie on his side, he leaned over and clamped his hand on the back of Stone's head, drawing Stone into a kiss that was light at first, but a low moan escaped Luke as soon as their lips touched, and he deepened the kiss, claiming the taste he'd said he wanted.

Stone parted his lips, giving a soft moan of his own as Luke kissed him. Luke tasted sweet, and Stone wanted more of him. "Move over," he growled against Luke's lips. "Since you don't mind."

Luke scooted back to make room for him. "Plenty of room in here for two."

Stone moved onto the bed and pulled the covers down so he could look at Luke's chest. He'd avoided peeking when he'd undressed Luke earlier, but he looked his fill now. He caressed Luke's pale skin, running his fingers though the crisp hair on Luke's chest. "You look good. Almost as good as you taste."

Luke's eyes were half-lidded, and he was practically purring at the touch of Stone's hand. "If you see anything you want, you sure enough can have it."

"That's good to know," Stone continued to caress Luke, pleased to know he was the one making Luke look like he was about to melt right into the mattress. He slid his hand lower, pushing the covers farther down so he could see if Luke was as aroused as he was. Apparently so, and Stone gave a little growl of satisfaction. "I think I see what I want."

Luke kicked the covers out of the way, and Stone wasn't the least bit surprised the man had no shame about baring himself. "It's all yours," Luke drawled. "You just tell me what you want to do with it." His expression turned more serious then, and he reached out to caress Stone's cheek tenderly. "I mean it. I ain't ashamed to say I find pleasure in both givin' and takin', and I'm willin' to do whatever you want me to do. I just want to make you happy, Stone. That's all."

"You do." Stone wasn't comfortable with saying things like that, but he owed it to Luke, especially when the look in Luke's eyes made his heart beat faster. A corner of his mind was worried, warning him these feelings were dangerous enough, but telling Luke how he felt would be disastrous. Stone ignored it, too mesmerized by the way Luke was touching him. Like he cared. Like Stone mattered. "Touch me. I want you to touch me."

Luke leaned in to nibble kisses along Stone's sharp jaw. "I've been wantin' to touch you since the day I laid eyes on you."

Luke claimed another kiss, this one deep and drugging, as he began unfastening the buttons on Stone's shirt, impatiently pushing the fabric out of the way so he could caress the smooth, bare skin beneath, seeming eager to stroke every inch he could reach.

The kiss was wonderful, but the slide of Luke's hand over his skin made Stone moan with need. It had been so long since anyone had touched him, and he was coming to life beneath Luke's caressing fingers. He wanted more; he wanted Luke to keep touching him until he died.

He wanted to touch, too, so he skimmed his hand along Luke's side, down to the sharp angle of his hip. Then he tugged, pulling Luke closer, wanting to feel Luke along every inch of him, sighing softly at the press of bare skin against bare skin.

Luke bit lightly at Stone's bottom lip and broke away. "You've got too many clothes on. It's hinderin' my attempts to touch you like I want."

Stone unfastened his trousers and quickly pushed them down and off. "There. Now you got no excuse for not givin' me what I want. And I want it all."

Luke's smile turned wicked as he skimmed his fingertips slowly down the length of Stone's torso, leaving a trail of fire along the way. The muscles in his abdomen quivered in response to the too-light touch, but Luke seemed determined to torment him.

"You want me to touch you, right?" Butter wouldn't melt in Luke's mouth, and his innocent look was belied by the devilish way he curled his fingers around Stone's hard cock. "Like this?"

"Yes!" Stone groaned the word, fisting his hands in the sheets as Luke touched him. He was breathing hard, and he had to force himself to keep still. He wanted to move, to feel Luke caressing him and driving him over the edge, but he didn't want it to be over too soon. He looked at Luke and licked his lips. "Yeah, like that."

Luke didn't seem to be in any hurry either, because he stroked Stone slowly, building up his need and then backing off again and again. He watched Stone's face avidly, seeming to enjoy the signs of pleasure he saw there.

"Tease." Stone bit out the word between clenched teeth, as Luke seemed determined to drive him mad. "You're goin' to kill me." He framed Luke's face between his hands. "I saw how you looked at me that day in the stable. Like you wanted to push me up against the wall and take me. I want to see you look at me like that again."

Luke brushed a kiss to Stone's palm. "That's just what I'll do right now if you want me to."

"I want you to. I want you to take me."

Luke rolled away long enough to rummage around in a drawer in the bedside table, and he pulled out a bottle of Neatsfoot oil, smiling sheepishly. "I've needed this a fair bit since you got here. You've kept me so wound up, I don't know how long I can hold out once I'm in you."

Stone couldn't help the satisfied smile that curved his lips at the thought of Luke wanting him so much that he had to take the edge off from time to time. He held out his arms, beckoning for Luke to come back, wanting to feel Luke against him. "Show me what you thought about doin' to me when you got all wound up."

Luke straddled Stone's hips and grabbed Stone's wrists, pinning them against the pillow over his head, the easygoing air replaced by pure need. He rocked his hips provocatively. "I thought about this. I thought about you beggin' me for more."

Stone Harrison wasn't the type of man to beg, but the sudden, fierce expression on Luke's face stole his breath and made him ache in ways he'd never felt before. The tone of Luke's voice sent a shiver down his spine, and Stone arched his back, need shooting through him like a bolt of lightning.

"Please, Luke." He cast his pride aside and begged, his voice full of need. "More. I need more."

"Oh God, Stone, so do I." Luke released Stone's wrists so he could grab the bottle of oil. "I need you right now, or I just might die."

"Then have me." Stone bucked his hips impatiently and grasped the bars of the iron headboard. "Don't worry about bein' gentle. Just give us what we both want!"

Uncorking the bottle, Luke poured a generous amount of oil into his palm, crooning softly and soothingly as he prepared Stone with gentle fingers despite Stone's demands. "I don't want to hurt you. It's been a while for you, I'm guessin', and I want this to be good. Nothin' but pleasure."

Stone tossed his head on the pillow, the touch of Luke's fingers and his words almost undoing him then and there. He was on fire, and he was ready to combust from pure need. He couldn't remember ever wanting anyone this badly before, and he looked at Luke, not hiding how desperate he was. "Damn it, Luke! Now!"

Finally, Luke poured out another dollop of oil and put the bottle aside, grinning wickedly down at Stone as he made a show of preparing himself. But all teasing ended as he settled Stone's legs over his shoulders and positioned himself, slowly easing his thick cock into Stone's pliant body.

"So good." Luke groaned, his fair skin growing flushed. "So perfect!"

"Perfect." Stone echoed the word, holding his breath as he adjusted to Luke's hard length within him. The way Luke filled him felt so damned good, and he wriggled impatiently, trying to pull Luke even deeper. "Move," he demanded.

Luke didn't hesitate to obey, setting a steady rhythm as he claimed Stone with deep, powerful thrusts, and Stone felt a jolt of pure pleasure every time Luke's cock rubbed against something inside him, making him whimper and moan. Luke curled his fingers around Stone's cock again, stroking him in sync with the rhythm of their bodies.

"Let go, boss," Luke murmured, gazing down at Stone with warm affection in his eyes. "I've got you."

Stone held Luke's eyes, wanting to give Luke exactly what he asked for. His body tightened as need coiled within him like a clock spring being wound, and then suddenly he cried out Luke's name as wave after wave of ecstasy crashed over and through him.

Luke's face was alight as he watched Stone avidly, and it seemed as if the waves of Stone's pleasure washed over him as well. He pounded into Stone hard and fast, and Stone moved with him, spurring him on. In mere moments, Luke surged deep and shuddered as he came.

Panting, he eased out and collapsed beside Stone, wrapping both arms around him and pulling him close, nuzzling his cheek. "That was worth the wait."

Stone felt a delicious lassitude stealing over him in the aftermath, and he sighed, enjoying the closeness and connection to Luke. It was an odd feeling in some ways, different from anything he'd felt before. "Glad you think so."

"Definitely." Luke caressed Stone's back from shoulder to hip in languorous strokes, seeming to enjoy the closeness as well. "It's good between us, just like I knew it would be."

Stone gave him a questioning look. "How could you know that?" he asked drowsily. "I tried not to let you see what I am."

Luke chuckled and gave him a warm squeeze. "I know you tried to hide from me, but you're too much like Priss for me not to see the truth. We're like salt and pepper. Different, but tasty together."

"Hmph." Stone gave a snort, not certain he liked that Luke could read him so easily. "You must be the pepper. I'm too boring for that."

"You're a lot of things, boss," Luke said softly, his voice full of affection as he stroked Stone's hair and back gently, soothing him into sleep. "But boring sure as hell ain't one of them."

Stone smiled, feeling more content than he had in longer than he could remember. There was something else, too, but he was too tired to put his finger on it. Instead he snuggled closer to Luke's warmth, and then sleep claimed him at last.

10

WHEN Luke awoke the next morning, it took him a moment to remember why he felt so uncommonly good, but then memories of the night before returned, and he smiled. Not about the part where he'd almost frozen to death in that sudden blizzard, but about what happened after with Stone. It seemed all that mortal peril had made Stone finally realize he wanted to do something about the powerful attraction other than deny it, which had led to a mighty good night for Luke indeed.

He frowned when he opened his eyes to see the sun was up and the bed was empty, and he wondered why Stone hadn't woken him. Snow or no snow, there were still chores to do, and Luke hauled himself out of bed, got a quick wash, and dressed in his warmest clothes.

Mary was in the kitchen, and she smiled at him when he walked in. "Mr. Harrison said I was to let you sleep as long as you wanted," she said, as if anticipating his first question, and she gazed at him with obvious concern. "He said you got caught in that blizzard last night."

"That I did, but Mr. Harrison came and fetched me out of it before any real harm was done. You didn't walk here today, did you?"

"No, my pa brought me in the sleigh. He's comin' for me before sunset."

"Good." Luke nodded approvingly. If Mary's father hadn't been planning to pick her up, Luke would have offered to carry her back to town himself.

"Mr. Harrison also said you wasn't to do no chores today." Mary's expression turned stern, and she wagged her finger at him. "You're to take the day off."

Luke was aghast at the mere idea. He hadn't taken a full day off that wasn't a Sunday in longer than he could remember, but if he didn't, Mary would tell Stone, and there was no telling what Stone might do if he disobeyed. Then again, he thought mischievously, it might be fun to find out.

But truth to tell, he was tired and achy still, and so after eating a late breakfast, he occupied himself with a little book work, and when that ran out, he tried reading until it put him to sleep for a couple of hours. By the time Mary went home that afternoon, Luke was getting antsy enough that he puttered around the kitchen, putting leftovers together for a nice dinner for Stone, even setting the table. He tried not to keep looking at the door to see if Stone was coming yet, but he couldn't help it; he was eager to see Stone again, eager to take him back to bed for more kissing and touching than they'd gotten to do last night. Tonight, they could take it nice and slow because they wouldn't be so desperate, and he could set about exploring and memorizing every inch of Stone's gorgeous body like he so wanted to do.

It wouldn't be easy to hide how he felt, not when he wanted to tell the whole world Stone Harrison was his man, but he'd manage it somehow when they were out where prying eyes might see. Here in the big house with Mary gone for the day, they were safe, and Luke intended to spend that evening and every other from now on showing Stone how good it could be and how much he was loved until maybe he started loving Luke right back.

It was full dark before the kitchen door opened and Stone stepped inside. His back to Luke, he took off his wet, muddy boots, and then he removed his coat and hat and put them on the pegs. Only then did he turn around, but he didn't meet Luke's eyes.

"We lost ten head in the pasture. Spent all day butchering 'em. I'm goin' to go clean up."

The loss of so many cattle was disappointing, but not surprising; the ranch had suffered worse losses over the years, and so Luke merely nodded acceptance of the news.

"If you want a bath, I'll heat up some water for you and scrub your back," he offered, giving Stone a playful grin.

Stone went very still, and then he raised his head, but he still didn't meet Luke's gaze. Instead he seemed to focus on a point somewhere over Luke's left shoulder, and when he spoke, his tone was wooden. "That ain't a good idea. It'd be best to forget that anything untoward happened."

Luke's stomach plummeted to his boots, and he stared at Stone, not wanting to believe what he was hearing. "'Tweren't nothing *untoward*," he protested, taking a step toward Stone and stretching out his hand beseechingly. "It was the best night of my life, and I don't want to forget it."

He paused, horrified by a thought that suddenly occurred to him. "Did I hurt you? I swear, I didn't mean to, and if I did, I'm awful sorry. You just tell me what it was I did wrong, and I won't never do it again. I'll do better next time, I promise." He was on the verge of begging, something he had never done before in his life, but for Stone, he was willing to throw his pride out the window. "Just give me another chance to make it good for you, *please*."

Stone took a step back, and Luke saw the betraying flush creeping into his cheeks. He shook his head. "You didn't hurt me. But there can't be a next time." Stone's voice was hoarse. "There shouldn't have been a *first* time. It's not your fault. It's mine. I'd been drinkin', and when that happens, I do things I shouldn't. I was feelin' guilty for almost gettin' you killed, and the bottle was there, and I… I was weak. I'm sorry, but you can put the blame on me."

Luke stared at Stone with growing dismay. As relieved as he was to know he hadn't hurt Stone, he almost wished that *had* been the problem. *That* he could fix. Flat-out denial was going to be harder to deal with.

"I don't understand. Why can't there be a next time? What we did wasn't wrong." He fell silent, thinking about what Stone had said, and he swallowed hard, fighting the heavy ball of ice forming in his guts. "Unless it didn't mean nothin' to you. Is that it? You felt bad, and I was convenient, and that's all there was to it?"

At last, Stone looked at him, eyes flying up and locking onto his, the shock and denial on his face telling Luke what he needed to know before Stone even opened his mouth. "No! It wasn't like that. I wish I could lie to you and say it was, because then you'd hate me, and it'd be over. It did mean somethin', and it *can't*. You know the way the world works, Luke. You've seen it. That's why you helped Priss. People talk, and that talk can ruin a person. The hands are already talkin' about us!" Stone frowned and shook his head. "All day I had to listen to them talkin' about me ridin' out to rescue you. I'm terrified they can see the truth about what we did on my face. It's been hard enough to hide what I am all these years, even with not lettin' anybody close. That's why we can't do this. It'd cost us both too much."

"I don't care!" Luke shook his head vehemently. "This ranch ain't worth givin' up happiness. Yeah, I helped Priss because I wanted her and Sarah to be safe and happy, but people talk more about women who don't act like they need a man more'n they talk about men, and you know it. It'd be easier for us, and we'd be careful, but even if people found out, so what? We could leave and start over somewhere else. I'd do it if it meant bein' with you."

He stopped short of blurting out *Because I love you*, not wanting to make himself look completely pathetic.

Stone's eyes were dark, and his lips twisted in bitterness. "It ain't as easy as you seem to think. You've been here on this ranch the whole time I've been wanderin' half the country, tryin' to find a place to call home. It ain't easy out there for men like us, Luke. I got a bullet through the shoulder that told me there're folks who wouldn't be satisfied with ridin' us out of town on a rail. They'd want to kill us for bein' what we are. You said this ranch was your home, and even as short a time as I've been here, it's become my home, too. I don't want to lose it. Takin' a drink last night was one of the most stupid things I've ever done, because it made me forget that."

Luke understood that line of reasoning, but understanding didn't make it hurt any less. He couldn't blame Stone for feeling that way, given Stone's past; he didn't know the whole story, of course, but what little Stone had revealed made it clear why Stone would value having a stable home.

"It ain't easy," he conceded, his shoulders slumping wearily. "I can't argue with that. I can't make you choose, either. I know havin' a home is important to you. It's important to me too, but not as important as bein' happy. Just bein' here ain't enough to make me happy or make this anything more than a house to live in. Can you tell me it's enough to make *you* happy?"

Stone frowned. "You said this was your home. That you want to stay. I'm not just thinkin' of myself in this. It's you too! Say we did go on, and we got run out of town. How long would it be before you started hatin' me for costin' you so much? We both have a responsibility to this place and to Priss. If we got run off, what happens to the ranch and to the hands? It's not as simple as just you and me. I ain't run out on a responsibility yet, Luke. My pa ran out on every job he ever had, and he ran out on us, too. I'd end up hatin' myself if I acted like him."

"I couldn't never hate you." Luke thought he understood what was going on, at least a little. He still didn't know if Stone felt anything for him, but whether Stone did or not, it didn't really matter because Stone had ghosts haunting him, the kind Luke didn't have. It would be easy for Luke to walk away from the ranch because it was just a place, and the hands would find work elsewhere, but for Stone, it was all tangled up with his pa, and that was a battle Luke wasn't sure he could fight, much less win. Stone had to do that himself.

"This is my home, and I want to stay, but more'n that, I want to be with you." He paused, debating how to continue. He could admit

70

how he felt and see if that made a difference, but he was feeling too battered, and he was pretty sure it wouldn't matter. Stone had made his choice, and he'd chosen the ranch, not Luke. "But if that offer ain't on the table, then I guess that's the end of it."

Stone nodded slowly. "I suppose it is. I'm sorry. I didn't mean for this to happen. I wouldn't blame you if you wanted to punch me in the face."

Luke mustered a smile from somewhere, his pride refusing to let him reveal more than he already had, especially not the fact that his heart was breaking. "No need to apologize. Like you said, we'll just forget anything untoward happened." He nodded respectfully and started heading for the stairs, desperate to escape. "Supper's in the kitchen if you want it. I'll see you in the mornin'." He stopped just short of adding *boss*, unable to voice what had become, for him, a term of endearment.

"'Night, Luke," Stone replied, his voice thick and hoarse.

Luke didn't reply, and he didn't look back, knowing if he did, he might do something stupid like begging Stone to reconsider. He didn't know if he could stay on the ranch after this, but he didn't want to think about it tonight. He wasn't the kind to act in haste, and he wasn't about to start now. He'd wait and watch and think, and then he'd make up his mind. But not tonight.

Tonight was for whiskey and sleep, and maybe if he was lucky, he wouldn't dream about Stone Harrison.

11

"'NIGHT, Mr. Harrison! Thanks for a great party! Merry Christmas!"

"Merry Christmas," Stone replied, waving as the last of the hands headed back toward the bunkhouse. Finally alone, he sagged against the wall with a sigh.

Normally he wasn't much for socializing, but he'd learned the Christmas Eve party was a tradition at the ranch, and his aunt had used the occasion to thank the hands for their hard work. Stone wasn't about to cancel something that meant so much to the men, so he'd played host, although he hadn't enjoyed it, because he felt a pang every time he set eyes on Luke.

Ever since that evening in the kitchen when he'd had to push Luke away, Stone had felt awful. He'd told Luke the truth, even though lying would have been a damned sight easier. He couldn't let Luke think that night had meant nothing to him. The trouble was, it had meant a hell of a lot more than he wanted to admit to Luke or anyone else. They both had too much to lose, and Stone couldn't stand to think of Luke being shot by an angry mob because of him. That was the worst part: knowing he could be responsible for Luke's death.

It had been awkward between them ever since, which was to be expected, but Stone missed Luke smiling and teasing him and calling him "boss." Now it was "sir," and that word made Stone cringe every time Luke said it. He wished he'd never taken that drink. He wished he'd never crawled into bed with Luke. Everything was wrong, now, and it was all Stone's fault because he'd given in to temptation.

He had no choice but to go on, and that meant he had something else to do tonight, something he actually *wanted* to do this time. He knew he couldn't make up for hurting Luke, but that didn't mean he couldn't try to make things better.

Stone headed to the kitchen, where he'd last seen Luke, and he cleared his throat as he caught sight of Luke making a beeline for the stairs. "I was wonderin' if you have a minute?"

Luke froze with his foot on the bottom step, obviously wanting to make his escape, but he turned to face Stone, giving him a friendly if somewhat impersonal smile. "Yes, sir. What can I do for you?"

"There's somethin' in the stable I need you to take a look at. Can you come with me?" he asked, trying to sound casual, but his heart ached over the new strain between them. He missed the comfortable ease they'd once shared.

"Is somethin' wrong?" Luke's expression turned concerned. "Ferdy didn't kick a hole in the stall again, did he?"

"No, nothin' like that. Just somethin' I want your opinion on. If you don't mind."

"No, sir, I don't mind." Luke got his coat from the peg and shrugged into it, and then he grabbed his hat. "Ready when you are."

Stone bundled up as well and headed out the door, his heart thudding so hard in his chest he wondered if Luke could hear it. He led the way across to the stable in silence, glad the wind was still for once, so they wouldn't be half frozen once they got there.

He opened the door for Luke and followed him inside, glad to see Shorty had left a lantern on as Stone had asked. He'd told Shorty he would be coming out to check on Daisy, the pregnant mare, before he went to bed, but in truth, he had a different purpose in mind.

He beckoned Luke to the side of Mist's stall. A blanket was draped over the top rail, covering something underneath. He looked at

Luke, feeling almost shy. "It's after midnight, so it's Christmas. I had somethin' I wanted to give you."

Luke's eyes widened slightly, and he shook his head. "You didn't have to. I didn't expect nothin'."

"I wanted to." He looked at Luke, silently begging him to understand. "I couldn't run this place without you. You've taught me everything I know, and I want to show you how much y—that means to me." He pulled the blanket off, revealing a brand new saddle, its rich leather gleaming in the low light. It was a working saddle, but there was fancy embossing on it with the initials "LR" worked into it.

Luke stared at the saddle, his jaw dropping in shock. "I can't take that! It's too much. It's…." He pressed his lips together and shook his head.

"Please." Stone rested his hand on the saddle, stroking the leather. "I want you to have it. If it helps, think of it from bein' from me and Priss. We both owe you more than we could repay."

Luke seemed to waver at that, and then he nodded slowly. He touched the fine leather, the barest brush of his fingertips, and Stone thought he saw a flash of sadness in Luke's eyes. "For Priss's sake and the ranch. I didn't do none of it expectin' repayment, though."

"I know that." Stone was relieved Luke had accepted the gift; he hoped the next part would go as smoothly. "But you've given a good chunk of your life to this ranch, and that means you're entitled to somethin' for it. I mean more'n just pay. Sure, the steady hands work hard, too, but they don't have the connection to the place you do. You didn't have to stay on after Priss died, and you didn't have to help me, but you did. A man has to have somethin' in his life that's his and his alone, more'n just the clothes on his back. I don't know how many times I'd have given up if Raider hadn't kept me goin'. That's why I'm givin' you Mist free and clear. She's already yours in your heart and hers. I just want to make it official."

It was probably the longest speech he'd ever made in his life, but Stone meant every word, and he watched Luke anxiously to see how he'd react.

74

Luke opened Mist's stall and went inside, gently stroking the mare's neck as he gazed at her in silence for a long minute or two. "I reckon you're right," he said at last. "A man does need somethin' of his own to care about. Somethin' that needs him too. It's right generous of you, sir. I'm mighty grateful."

Luke's words sent a shaft of pain through Stone. He wished Luke could feel that way about *him*, that things weren't such a mess between them, and the world was a different place where they didn't care what two men or two women wanted to do together. It had been so hard to tell Luke they couldn't be together, and now Stone found himself wishing he could take that risk and damn the consequences.

"You don't have to be grateful." Stone kept his hands clenched at his sides so he didn't touch Luke the way he wanted to. "You deserve a hell of a lot more. I just—" He clamped his mouth shut, horrified he'd nearly blurted out that he wished he could give himself to Luke.

"You just what?" Luke turned to face Stone at last, his expression somber. "You feel so badly about what happened you've got to make it up to me somehow? Well, you don't. I'm a grown man, and I can take my lumps like a man." A stubborn frown creased his brow, which was an unusual sight for someone as easygoing as Luke. "I ain't plannin' to leave neither, if that's what you're worried about. I thought about it at first," he admitted, "but this ranch is my responsibility too, and I can't just up and leave no more than you can unless you decide to make me go."

Stone wanted to blurt out that Luke had it wrong, and he wasn't trying to make up for anything, but he bit back the words. "I'd never make you go. I can count on one hand the number of folks I can trust and have a couple of fingers left over, but I know I can depend on you. Maybe I don't know how to say things sometimes, but I thought I could show you."

Luke released a long, slow sigh, and the stubborn frown faded into wistfulness. He opened his mouth as if to speak, but then shut it again with a snap, seeming to think better of it. He gazed steadily at Stone for a long time before saying anything.

"You can still count on me," he said. "I'll do what's best for the ranch. Not just out of respect for Priss' memory, but for you, too. You got somethin' to prove to the world, and I'll help you prove it."

There was a sudden knot in his throat, and Stone lowered his gaze. "Thank you." His voice was hoarse, but there wasn't much he could do about that. He'd known Luke meant too much to him, but now he realized he'd gone and fallen in love with the man, which was probably the most foolish thing he'd ever done in his life. Especially since he couldn't let Luke find out how he felt.

Moving into the stall, Stone ran his hand along Mist's flank, wishing he could touch Luke instead. "I got the papers signed sayin' she's yours. Not that she didn't already know that. Didn't you, *asaákira?*" Mist turned to look at him, and he smiled. "*Acikskaawiraah, Kicpiíru'.*"

Luke shot him a puzzled look. "What'd you say?"

"I told her to take care of you and called her by her Pawnee name. *Kicpiíru'* means light rain or mist."

"That makes it sound real pretty," Luke said, his expression shifting from puzzled to curious. "Who taught you?"

Normally Stone didn't talk about his family, but he wanted to tell Luke. "My ma. She was half Pawnee. People called her Tara, but her name was *Áwataaru*—brightness."

Luke simply nodded, not seeming either surprised or repulsed by the revelation. "I figured you had some Indian blood. It don't matter to me," he added quickly. "I ain't the type to hate anyone for the color of their skin. Far as I'm concerned, ain't no man my enemy unless he's tryin' to kill me for no good reason. Then I'm goin' to feel a little less kindly toward him."

"That's sensible." Stone was pleased Luke didn't care about his origin, but he hadn't expected Luke to be put off, as easygoing and accepting as Luke was. He was even more pleased they were having a normal conversation, one in which Luke wasn't calling him "sir" every five minutes; he was coming to truly hate that word. "Well, I should get back to the house, I guess." He smiled hesitantly. "Merry Christmas, Luke."

"Thanks." Luke offered a half-smile in return, but it was a far cry from the open, easy smiles that had been noticeably missing for the past couple of weeks. "Oh, I got you somethin' too. It's back at the house. It's nothin' much. Not like this." He glanced over at Mist's stall.

"You did?" Stone's eyebrows climbed to his hairline, but the idea that Luke thought enough of him to get him a present made him unreasonably happy. "Thank you. That was mighty kind of you."

Luke glanced away, appearing embarrassed, and a slight flush rose in his cheeks. "It's nothin', really."

"No one's given me a present in longer'n I can remember. That's enough without me even knowin' what it is."

"I guess you can have it tonight if you want it." Luke slid his hands into his back pockets. "It's just somethin' I thought might be useful."

Stone smiled, wishing he could do something more to show Luke how grateful he was. But what he wanted to do was out of the question, so he patted Mist affectionately instead. "Ready to go back to the house?"

"Sure." Luke stepped out of the stall and closed it after Stone. He set off toward the house, walking beside Stone but keeping a careful distance. Once they were inside, he headed upstairs, and Stone heard him walking around. When he returned a few minutes later, he was carrying a small package wrapped in plain brown paper, which he held out to Stone.

"Here you go."

Stone took the package, examining it for a moment. He remembered when he'd been small, and his mother had managed to save up enough money to buy him gifts for either his birthday or Christmas. He'd always been so excited, and he felt an echo of his boyish delight as he held Luke's present in his hands. He smiled, almost hating to open it and end the anticipation, but Luke was waiting.

He untied the string and carefully unfolded the paper from around the box.

The wood had a beautiful brown finish, sanded and stained, and Stone ran his hand over it before he lifted the lid. Inside, on a bed of black fabric, was a gleaming black fountain pen with a gold tip and top clip. Stone drew in a breath in surprise and looked at Luke. "Thank you. It's the nicest thing anyone's ever given me."

"It's just a pen," Luke replied, still seeming abashed. "I thought you could use one of your own now that you're a landowner."

"Yeah." Stone knew he was probably grinning like an idiot, but he couldn't help it. "Most of the ranchers I worked for had pens, but they weren't as nice as this. Even Mr. Stevenson's, and he was right proud of his. Always wore it in his shirt pocket when he went to town, in case he had to sign anything. Thank you, Luke. It's perfect. I'll use it proudly."

"You're welcome." Luke seemed on the verge of saying something else, but instead, he took a step back. "I'm glad you like it."

"I do." Stone nodded, closing the box and resisting the urge to stroke the wood again. He looked at Luke from beneath his lashes. "I guess I should get to bed. You're to take the day off tomorrow, all right? I've got the chores."

For a moment, it looked like Luke might protest, but in the end, he didn't outright refuse, although he didn't look pleased either. "I suppose. I just had a whole day off, though, and I don't know what to do with myself without somethin' to do."

"You could break in that new saddle. See how you and Mist like it."

"I reckon I could." Luke nodded and turned toward the stairs. "Good night." He paused and then he added, "Merry Christmas."

"Merry Christmas." Stone watched Luke go up the stairs, wishing wistfully he had the right to go with him and spend the night making them both happy. But that was just a dream he'd have to keep to himself. He was far too old to believe Christmas wishes ever came true.

78

12

"SO THAT'S almost six thousand calves we're expecting." Stone looked down at the neatly totaled numbers on the sheet of paper in front of him, feeling a sense of accomplishment. A rancher never knew exactly how many of his cows had ended up pregnant until it got close to birthing time, but when the welcome warmth of spring finally arrived, it appeared Copper Lake had been lucky.

He glanced toward the other end of the table, where Luke was looking over his own set of papers. Luke had been lean when they first met, but he seemed to have lost weight, along with the tan he'd had the previous fall, leaving him looking thin and pale. But those weren't the only things that were different, and Stone knew it. Even the hands had noticed and commented on the changes in Luke over the winter; he was still friendly and easygoing, but he was quieter and kept to himself more, as if some of the light had gone out of him, and he didn't smile as much or joke as often.

It gave Stone a pang to know it was his fault Luke had changed, and he'd spent more than a few hours by himself, brooding about the situation and wondering how to change it. But try as he might, he didn't see a way he could give Luke what he wanted—and what he wanted himself—without risking both their lives and losing everything they'd worked for. It was almost enough to drive a man to drink, but that's what had gotten them both in this situation in the first place.

Forcing himself to keep his mind on work, Stone tapped on his paper. "Looks like we're goin' to need some more hands. How many do you want to hire? If we start out early, maybe we can get the better ones."

"I'd say at least eight or ten," Luke replied, glancing up from his work briefly. "Maybe as many as a dozen if we look to be busy. If we don't need them to work with the cattle, we can ask them to help out at the mine."

Stone nodded. "Sounds fine. We can send an ad to the Reno paper, if there ain't enough men local."

There was a knock on the kitchen door, and Stone looked up. "Wonder who that is?"

Luke shrugged, not looking up this time. "Must be one of the hands. Anyone else'd go to the front door."

"True." Stone rose and went to the door, opening it enough to look out without letting too much of the cold February air in. It was getting on toward evening, and since it was Sunday, the hands had been off all day, but it was always possible one of them needed something.

When Stone saw who stood on the back porch, he stared in utter surprise. "Little Sam? Is that really you?"

"Yeah, it's me." The young man Stone had last seen on the Circle J Ranch in Texas grinned up at him. "Didn't I tell you I was goin' to come out here and ask you for a job?"

"Yeah, you did," Stone acknowledged, shaking his head. Little Sam had been happy for Stone's inheritance—as had the Stevensons, who were the only other people Stone had told—but Little Sam had been wistful, too, since he couldn't afford to leave the Circle J and follow Stone on what Little Sam was convinced would be a grand adventure. He'd sworn he was going to come to Nevada as soon as he could, but Stone had been certain the day he left Yellow Knife was the last time he'd see Sam. Realizing he'd been staring, he stepped back and opened the door. "Come on in."

"Only for a minute," Sam said, stepping inside the warm kitchen. He glanced in Luke's direction. "Sorry if I'm interruptin', Stone, but I wanted to get here before you'd done all your hirin' for the spring. You're hirin', ain't you? Or know someone who might be?"

"Of course I'm hirin'." Stone shook his head in exasperation. Trust someone as young as Sam to take off all the way from Texas to Nevada without knowing if he'd have a job when he got there. He clapped Sam on the shoulder. "Luke, this here's Sam Thompson, but everyone calls him Little Sam. Little Sam, this is my foreman, Luke Reynolds."

Luke had abandoned his work at last, apparently finding their conversation more interesting, and he was watching the two of them with a faint frown. "Howdy," he said, although he sounded less friendly than he usually did to new folks.

"Mr. Reynolds, sir." Little Sam flushed under Luke's regard. "Pleased to meet you."

Stone frowned as well, wondering if something was wrong. "Little Sam was workin' on the Circle J when I got there and proceeded to make a nuisance of himself."

"Aw...." Sam shook his head in embarrassment. "I wasn't that bad! Besides, you needed a friend, didn't you?" He looked at Luke, as if anxious to explain himself. "Stone barely talked to anyone, and folks said I never shut up, so I guess it made sense I talked to him."

"I guess it did," Luke replied, fixing Stone with an inscrutable look. "Sounds to me like you got yourself a habit of pickin' up men who like to run their mouth at you, Mr. Harrison."

"Yeah, maybe I do." Stone still wasn't certain what was going through Luke's mind, but Luke sure didn't run his mouth anymore. He looked at Sam and smiled slightly. "If you're goin' to work for me, there better be less talkin' and plenty of workin'."

"Oh! Yeah, sure!" Sam nodded vigorously. "I know you're the boss now, Stone. But I guess I should call you Mr. Harrison?"

"We were hands together, so you can still call me Stone." He wagged his finger under Sam's nose. "But no tale tellin', you got me? And I ain't treatin' you any different from the other hands. I won't have no one sayin' you get away with anything because you knew me before, understand?"

"Right! I'm awful glad to be here." The irresistible grin Sam was known for split his face. "I always did want to see more than Texas, though so far all I've seen is a lot of snow. But the mountains look right pretty." He paused and bit his lip, looking at Stone hopefully. "Are the girls in these parts pretty, too?"

Luke flicked his gaze to Sam, his eyes widening, and then he leaned back in his chair, seeming to relax a little. "I reckon we've got our share of pretty gals in Serenity," he said. "I can introduce you around after church some time, if you want. I know who's single and who's got a steady beau already."

Sam smiled at Luke as though he'd just been offered a thousand dollars. "That's mighty nice of you, Mr. Reynolds! There weren't so many girls in Yellow Knife as would look at a cowboy like me."

Stone couldn't help snorting. "You mean there weren't so many girls who hadn't heard all your nonsense already." He ruffled Little Sam's hair. It was good to see the young man, if for no other reason than it helped him feel like he hadn't messed up every friendship in his life. "Go on, then. You can take your horse to the barn and get it settled, and the bunkhouse is out back. If you ain't had supper, I know Charlie keeps soup on for the hands all day on Sunday."

"Thanks, Stone! And it was nice to meet you, Mr. Reynolds." Little Sam nodded, and then took off out the door like an eager puppy ready to explore.

Stone walked to the back door and closed it, shaking his head. "Durn fool kid," he muttered.

"Looks like he likes you well enough," Luke said, turning back to his paperwork.

"Never did understand why." Stone returned to the table and took his seat. He didn't look down at his papers, however, taking a moment to study Luke, who had been uncharacteristically aloof until Sam had asked about girls. Stone was pretty sure he knew what Luke had been

82

thinking, and he felt he owed Luke some reassurance, no matter how uncomfortable it made him to give it.

"There ain't goin' to be no one from my past showin' up. Least not in the way you were obviously thinkin' about Sam. I don't want you thinkin' I won't take up with you, but I'd take up with someone else. There ain't never been anyone like that except for one man who was kind to me, a long time ago, and he was relieved to see the last of me when I left."

Luke went still for a moment before responding quietly. "You don't owe me no explanations. Your business is your business, not mine."

Stone's heart sank at the way Luke was continuing to shut him out. There was a gulf between them he didn't know how to get across except for the one way that would surely mean the ruin of them both. He just wished he could make Luke understand.

"Maybe I feel like I do owe you somethin', like respect of your feelin's. Maybe my respect ain't much, and maybe it ain't what you want, but I ain't plannin' to treat you like what you think don't matter." Stone rose, feeling like the walls were closing in on him. "I'll go introduce Sam to the others."

Luke pressed his lips together, as if to keep himself from saying more; instead he nodded curtly. "All right. I'll stay here and get some more work done."

Stone looked at him once more and then turned away, putting on his coat and hat. He wasn't good with words, and he didn't know what to say to make things better. So instead, he fell back into the silence he knew and trusted, and he left the warm kitchen, which seemed colder than the night outside without the warmth of Luke's smile.

13

"YEAH, boss, get 'em! Show 'em how it's done!"

Stone grinned at Shorty, who was waving his hat as Stone and Raider went after a calf who seemed determined to avoid being caught. Stone barely had to tell his horse what to do; after so many years together, he and Raider were in tune with each other and with the job they were doing.

The lasso was in his hand, and as Raider gained on the calf, Stone whipped it around his head and neatly tossed it over the young steer's neck. Raider stopped at once, and Stone secured the rope, dismounted, and hurried to flip the protesting calf onto its side, swiftly binding its legs with the slack of the rope.

"Not rodeo-pretty, but that'll do." Another hand, Brent Fields, came over with the branding iron. He marked the bawling calf on its flank and nodded to Stone. "That's about it for this batch, boss."

"Good." Stone clapped the cowboy on his shoulder, and then he released the calf, which ran off at once toward the rest of the herd, bawling in protest. Stone began to coil his rope in neat circles. "Let's finish up and get home, then." He started back toward Raider, pausing as he caught sight of Luke standing off to one side, looking far more handsome than any man had a right to be.

At that, Luke ambled over, touching the brim of his hat as he approached. "Didn't want to interrupt a man with rope in his hand and a hot brand nearby," he said, which was about as close to the kind of teasing he'd once plagued Stone with as he got these days. Unfortunately, the image of throwing a lasso around Luke and pulling him to the ground was not doing much to help Stone get on with his responsibilities.

Brent grinned at the two of them. "Yeah, Luke, the boss gets caught up in his work. Never seen a man so driven. Sometimes we think he's tryin' to work himself to death."

"Quit jawin' and get home to your dinner," Stone ordered gruffly, but not unkindly, and Brent chuckled and trotted over to the other cowboys, who were gathering the brands and dousing the fire. Stone raised one eyebrow at Luke. "You done for the day?"

"Yep. Mary sent me to make sure y'all didn't work too long and miss supper. You know how she is when you let her fried chicken get cold."

"I sure don't want to get her riled up." Stone tied his lariat onto his saddle and took Raider's reins, walking beside Luke as they made their way to where Mist was quietly grazing beneath a tree. Dusk was falling, but fortunately, the days were getting longer as they headed deeper into March. It had turned into a warm spring after the short but bitterly cold winter, and Stone was enjoying working outdoors again.

He waited while Luke mounted, and they rode in silence toward home. For all the awkwardness between them at times, Stone counted it a good thing Luke hadn't moved out of the ranch house. That would have been simply too much for Stone to take.

When they arrived, there was a strange buggy with a pair of matched black horses sitting in front of the house. It was a fancy rig, but Stone didn't recognize it as belonging to anyone from town.

He glanced at Luke. "Seems we have company. Any idea who it could be?"

Luke shook his head, looking as puzzled as Stone felt. "I ain't never seen a rig as fancy as that around here."

"Huh." Stone frowned as he dismounted and led Raider toward the stable. "Let's get one of the hands to take care of the horses, and we'll go find out what's going on."

After Mist and Raider were turned over to one of the wranglers, Stone and Luke made their way to the house. "Let's go in through the kitchen," Stone said, heading to the door. "I want to find out from Mary what's goin' on before we meet whoever it is."

Luke nodded and followed Stone inside. "Good idea."

Mary rushed over as soon as they entered. "Mr. Harrison, you have a visitor," she said, keeping her voice low, but Stone could hear the anxiousness in her tone. "I didn't know what to do, so I put him in the parlor to wait. I hope that's all right."

Stone smiled reassuringly at her. "That's fine, Mary. Don't worry. Who is it?"

Mary smoothed her hands down the front of her apron, and Stone noticed suddenly that her cheeks were pink. "He said he's your cousin, James. He's quite the fancy gentleman, ain't he? And so handsome!"

"Oh." Stone blinked at that, and then he looked at Luke, not sure what to think. "I ain't never heard of a cousin James. Did Priss have some other nephew I don't know about?"

"Not that I know of," Luke replied, his brows snapping together in a frown. "Not on the Harrison side, anyway. I don't know much about the Rivers side. Mr. Rivers had already passed on by the time I started workin' here, and she didn't talk much about his folks."

"Huh." Stone shrugged and hung his hat on the peg by the door. He didn't bother to wash up; he hadn't asked for a visitor, and he'd just worked a full day and expected to come home for his supper. Whoever this James person was could take Stone as he was or turn right around and go back to wherever he'd come from. "Well, let's see what this is all about." He looked at Luke hopefully. "Mind comin' with me? You know I'm no good with meetin' new folks."

"If you want me to." Luke glanced down at himself, and Stone imagined he was thinking he was unfit to meet new folks as well.

"If he expected to take supper with the president, he should have said he was comin'. This is our place. Hold your head up and be proud." He patted Luke's shoulder and headed toward the parlor.

"*Your* place," Luke muttered from behind him, but there wasn't time to debate the issue before they reached the parlor and this James fellow spotted them, dropping whatever he'd been looking at on the rolltop desk and smiling broadly at them.

"Dare I hope one of you fine gentlemen is my cousin Stone?" he asked, stepping forward with his hand outstretched. Stone noticed his skin was lily white, and there were no callouses on his slender fingers.

Stone frowned. "Fine gentleman" was a better description of this man with his fancy clothes and neatly combed hair. He was almost as tall as Stone but with a slender build, and Stone could see what had Mary's knickers all knotted up. Blond-haired and blue-eyed, James had the type of elegant good looks that practically shouted "city slicker" to Stone. Still, he couldn't be rude, since a man couldn't help where he came from, and Stone nodded as he stepped forward.

"I'm Stone Harrison." Stone clasped the man's hand and shook it firmly, unsurprised to find James' grip was weak and his skin as soft as it looked. "And you are?"

"James Rivers," the man replied, flashing another charming smile. "I'm your cousin, albeit by marriage. My father and your aunt's husband were brothers."

"I see." Stone frowned, not quite seeing how that made them related any more than any other two strangers, but city folk had different thoughts on things. "This is my foreman, Luke Reynolds. Luke ran the ranch for my aunt the last few years."

"Nice to meet you." Luke offered his hand, and James took it with less charm and enthusiasm.

"A pleasure," James said tersely, before turning his attention back to Stone. "I apologize for not contacting you sooner. I would have written to inform you of my arrival, but you know how unreliable the post can be. Besides, family doesn't stand on ceremony."

Stone frowned, not caring for the way this James fellow seemed to dismiss Luke as though he wasn't anyone important. "I wouldn't know." He crossed his arms over his chest. "Ain't had no family for a long time. What can I do for you, Mr. Rivers?"

"*We're* family!" James spread his hands and smiled widely. "It's a sad fact of life that the number of surviving family members dwindles as one grows older, and I've suffered too many losses of late. I'd like to cultivate strong relationships with those who remain, and that includes you, of course."

"Me?" Stone wasn't sure how to respond to that. He'd never had anyone seek him out to claim kinship with him before. Well, other than Priss leaving him the ranch, but that was different. "Oh. Well. That's nice of you." He glanced sidelong at Luke, looking for a clue as to how to react to this fine speech.

"Have you found a place to stay yet, Mr. Rivers?" Luke asked, sounding polite, but not the least bit warm and welcoming.

"Indeed I have not," James replied, still looking at Stone. "I was hoping I might prevail upon my cousin to let me stay here. It would make getting to know one another so much easier, don't you think?"

Frankly, Stone would rather have let his "cousin" stay in town with everyone else who wasn't a part of the ranch, but it would be powerfully rude to send him packing, and since Luke had asked the question, Stone felt like he had no choice at all.

"I suppose so. I'll have Mary make up the front room and move Priss's stuff to the housekeeper's room." He had no doubt Mary would be ecstatic about their unexpected guest, but Stone was certain she'd be the only one.

James gave him a quizzical look at that. "I remember there being a guest room. That's where I stayed before. Has that changed?"

"I took that room when I moved in, since I felt wrong disturbin' my aunt's things." Stone shrugged, refusing to elaborate. "Luke has the other room on the front, so unless you want Sarah's old room by the kitchen, that's about all we got." He didn't mention the foreman's house, because he wasn't going to say anything that might send Luke packing.

"Your *foreman* stays *here*?" James appeared on the verge of being scandalized. "Well, I hope you have him paying rent for the privilege, at least."

"'Scuse me?" Stone's jaw dropped as he stared at his supposed cousin, unable to believe what he was hearing. "Now look here, Mr. Rivers, I am willin' to give you a chance on account of you claimin' kinship, but you best be understandin' how it works 'round here. A man who's proved himself don't have to pay for nothin' in my book, and if it weren't for Luke, there wouldn't *be* a ranch. If you're so keen on family, where were you when Priss was sick and needed help? I feel bad enough not bein' here for her, and I didn't even know I had an aunt. So you best be showin' Luke the respect he deserves for doin' more for Priss than her kin by blood or marriage ever did, or I'll be takin' back that invitation." He stared at James, not blinking. He wasn't going to listen to anyone badmouth Luke.

James' smile turned conciliatory. "I'm terribly sorry, cousin," he said in a tone that Stone wasn't entirely convinced was sincere. "I didn't mean to cause offense to you or your foreman here. I'm sure he's been invaluable. Of course, I'll take whatever accommodations you have available, and I'm grateful for them."

Stone nodded curtly. "Well, then. Mary has supper ready, and we've been workin' since sunup, so if you're of a mind to join us for a meal, we're eatin' in the kitchen. Mary can make up that room in the meantime." He turned and looked at Luke. "That suit?"

"Yes, sir, it suits me fine," Luke replied, turning his back just enough to shut James out of their conversation without quite being rude about it.

"It suits me as well," James interjected smoothly.

Stone nodded and headed for the kitchen. "Mary, we have a guest for supper." He moved to the sink and began to prime the pump with suppressed aggression. He washed his hands, telling himself he needed to calm down and get his temper under control. James Rivers had

89

gotten under his skin, but Stone knew he was no longer in a position where he could deck the man for being a jackass and get away with it. He probably should have sent the man packing at once, but it was too late to do anything about it now, except hope James kept his visit brief.

"Oh!" Mary's eyes widened, and she smiled bashfully at James. "I'll set another place, sir."

"That'll be fine." Stone dried his hands and headed to the table. "Then if you don't mind clearin' Priss's room, Mr. Rivers will be stayin' with us for a spell."

Mary was beaming at that, but Stone felt weary. He had someone in his house whom he didn't much care for, forcing him to be social, and for some reason, the whole situation with Luke was suddenly eating at him again, probably because he had really wanted to punch Mr. Smarmy-Pants Rivers right in his elegant nose for insulting Luke. But he had to get through this somehow, so he clenched his jaw and took his seat at the table.

James claimed a seat without waiting to see where Luke would sit, lounging with indolent grace and casting flirtatious smiles at Mary as she served them.

"It all looks delicious," he said, but as soon as Mary was out of the room, he added, "Of course, it's quite different from what I'm accustomed to. I'd forgotten how simple and unsophisticated the fare is out here."

Stone looked at Luke instead of James in an effort to keep himself from saying something rude. "Mary's cookin' suits us just fine."

"It'll suit me just fine, too," James replied, showing little reluctance to dig in. "Although you really must visit me sometime and let me show you around Boston. You'd be amazed at all the advances we have in technology these days, and it does take such a long time to bring civilization out west."

"We have indoor plumbin' and an icebox here," Luke spoke up at last, lifting his chin proudly.

"Do you?" James turned to him with an indulgent smile. "How grand."

Stone normally didn't talk much at supper, but something about this city slicker was pestering him. "It's enough for us," he said, taking a sip of the cold well water in his glass. "Trappin's don't make a man, and we've got all the civilization we want." He caught Luke's eye and kept his face perfectly straight. "I don't reckon we've had a witch burnin' in at least a month."

"There was that near miss when old Mrs. Dawkins showed up in church with a wart on her nose, but other than that, yeah, I'd say at least a good month," Luke replied, his expression admirably deadpan.

James laughed heartily, but somehow the sound rang false. "Touché, gentlemen. I stand corrected."

"Copper Lake Ranch is right comfortable," Stone replied. "Maybe we don't know much better, but it's home. That's all that really matters, leastwise to me."

"Of course. I'm sure it's quite nice to have somewhere to settle down in relative comfort this far from civilization," James replied. "I would miss the amenities offered by city life, but I can already appreciate the rustic charms of this area."

Stone nodded, but didn't say anything. Even when James said something complimentary, there seemed to be another meaning underneath his words. People like that annoyed Stone, and nothing he said was going to make a difference at all to this man. It was best to save his breath.

He finished up his third piece of fried chicken and wiped his hands on his napkin. "I think Mary made apple pie." He pushed back his chair and looked at Luke. "You want a cup of coffee with it?"

"I'll get it." Luke glanced at James, who looked disapproving.

"No, I'm up." Stone didn't care a fig what Mr. James Rivers thought. He crossed to the stove and fetched the coffee pot Mary had left out to keep warm, bringing it to the table and filling Luke's cup. "How about you, cousin? Coffee?"

"Since you're up," James drawled, holding out his cup.

Stone filled it—resisting the urge to dump the whole pot in James's lap—then poured his own cup before setting the pot in the middle of the table. He picked up the used plates, stacking them by the sink, and he brought the pie and three clean plates back to the table.

He took his seat and served a piece of pie to Luke and James before serving himself. Taking a bite of the pie, he glanced at Luke. "I need to make a supply run into town tomorrow. You want to go with me, or should I take Shorty?"

Luke poked at the apple pie with his fork, seeming to have little appetite for it, and kept his eyes on his plate. "I've got some work to do in the north pasture."

"I'd be glad to accompany you, cousin," James spoke up. "I'd love to see if Serenity has changed at all since the last time I was here."

Stone was disappointed Luke didn't want to go with him, but he was downright displeased at the thought of taking this new cousin of his instead. There didn't seem to be any help for it; hopefully James would decide Serenity and Copper Lake were too backward and "rustic" for his city tastes and leave soon.

"Sure, if you want," he agreed slowly. "I'm leavin' at eight." There was something wrong with Luke, and Stone wanted to know what it was. He was determined to have a private word with him before bed and find out what was going on.

"Of course." James nodded, seeming unperturbed by the early hour. "We can take my rig, if you like. It's one of the finest models ever made, and you really should have the experience at least once. Speaking of which, my horses need tending. Do you have a stable boy for that?"

Stone wasn't impressed that James didn't tend his own horses, but by now, he wasn't surprised. "You can take your rig, if you want, but I'm goin' to take the buckboard. I doubt you want sacks of flour and sugar in your nice buggy." He cleaned his plate and then stood up again. "If you want to go to the parlor, I'll get one of the wranglers to see to your horses. Luke, I want to discuss our chores for tomorrow."

James didn't look too happy over being dismissed, but he smiled and murmured, "Of course, cousin," before excusing himself and returning to the parlor. Once they were alone, Luke pushed back his chair and stood up, regarding Stone warily.

"If you aim to make me go into town with you and Dandy Jim, I'll want a day and a half's wages at least."

"No, I wasn't goin' to make you," Stone replied, running a hand through his hair in agitation. "I'd rather not go myself, truth be told, but it's too late now. Come on, let's step outside. I need to see his horses don't end up standin' hitched all night."

Once they were out in the cool, crisp evening air, Stone turned to Luke, his expression earnest. "Look, I know things ain't been right between us since that night, but I'm tryin', and I know you are too. But I can tell there's more goin' on now. What is it, Luke? If this city slicker makes you uncomfortable, I'll send him packin', cousin or no. I ain't got much use for him myself, but I'm tryin' to do what's right by Priss."

Luke stared at Stone, seemingly shocked into silence, but then he shook his head and turned away. "I don't much like your cousin, no more'n you do, I reckon, but there ain't no need to run him off right yet." He gazed at Stone, and Stone could see the inner battle he was waging before he finally exclaimed, "I don't get it, that's all. I thought you was worried about people talkin'! I guess it's different if they're talkin' about how noble you are, standin' up for the help to some fancy fool they won't like none anyway."

"What?" Stone was shocked, Luke's words jabbing into him like a knife. It hurt like hell Luke could think such a thing of him, when all he'd tried to do was fight for him. "I'd've stood up for you, no matter if it was him or the preacher or anyone else sayin' such things about you. Not because I care what people think about me, but because I won't have you disrespected when you ain't done nothin' to deserve it. And the problem ain't what people talk about. It's what they do when they finish talkin'. There's worse things than bein' run out of town on a rail. Like gettin' shot or strung up from a tree for not bein' what they think

93

you should be. I couldn't live with myself if you got hurt because of me." He shook his head, cold emptiness filling him. "If you could think such things about me, I reckon you don't really know me at all."

With that, he turned and headed toward the stable, wishing the earth would open up and swallow him whole. It'd be a damn sight easier than living with knowing the person he cared about most in the world thought he was lower than a snake.

He heard Luke's footsteps as he hurried to catch up with him, and felt Luke's hand on his arm to stop him—the first time Luke had voluntarily touched him since their one night together.

"I'm sorry," Luke said, lowering his hand quickly. "I didn't mean it like that. I just…." He blew out a sharp sigh. "It ain't easy. You give me fancy gifts and go on about how much you trust me, and you get madder'n a wet hen at Dandy Jim 'cause of how he treats me, but for all of that, you won't share my bed. I know it's 'cause you're scared of what could happen, but it don't make things any easier on me to know I've got to listen to all that and still keep my distance like it don't mean nothin'." He frowned and leveled an accusatory finger at Stone. "And if you think it won't make tongues wag if you keep actin' like a protective beau like you did tonight, you're foolin' yourself. Dandy Jim may be soft, but he ain't stupid or blind."

Stone would have liked nothing better at that moment than to push Luke up against the wall and kiss him senseless, but that was out of the question. He was beginning to wonder if it would be easier to stop fighting and let it happen. At least he and Luke would be happy for a while, until it all fell apart.

"I take your meanin'," he replied with a sigh. "And I ain't tryin' to make anything hard on you. I just hate seein' a man who ain't fit to lick your boots actin' like he's better'n you, sayin' things to try to make you feel bad. He may be Priss's nephew by marriage, but I can't claim that man as kin. Maybe tomorrow I can get him to go right back east in his fancy rig and leave us alone."

"I wouldn't mind seein' the dust of his shoes, that's for sure." Luke glanced back at the big house with an uncharacteristic scowl.

Stone nodded. "Well, I'd best get Ray or Jake to get his rig taken care of. I don't recall the last time I met anybody I had so little use for."

"You ain't goin' to get any disagreement out of me. At least Mary's taken a likin' to him, or else we'd be in a mess of trouble. Then again, maybe havin' to eat Charlie's cookin' instead of hers might make him decide to head back to Boston a lot quicker."

"That's worth considerin'." Stone smiled slightly. At least Luke was joking with him a little again, which was better than silence. "I should ask Mary if she can make a humble pie. I think he needs to eat a whole one by himself."

"If he didn't turn up his nose at it." Luke took a step back, eyeing Stone. "Anyway, I guess I'd better be gettin' back to the house."

"Right." Stone repressed a desire to sigh at the visible retreat. "I'll be in directly. I won't abandon you to our 'guest'."

"He ain't *our* guest," Luke retorted. "He's *your* guest. That ain't my house, this ain't my ranch, and I ain't family. I'm the foreman, that's all."

Stone looked at him. "I'll try to remember that." Then he turned and headed toward the stable. Whatever awaited him when he went back to the house, he felt certain he wasn't going to like it much at all.

14

IF ANYONE had asked Luke if he was happy before Stone came along, he would have said yes. He'd *thought* he was happy at the time, because he had a place to live, a job, and a little family. He didn't own the house he lived in, but he had a room he didn't have to share with anyone else, and for him, that was pure luxury. Looking back, he knew he'd only been content, which wasn't the same thing as being happy. He'd learned the difference the night he spent with Stone. That was when he'd learned what real, bone-deep happiness felt like.

Since then, he'd been struggling to get back to content, but he hadn't made it there yet; he wasn't sure he ever would. Sometimes, he thought leaving Copper Lake was the best answer for both of them, but he knew he would carry Stone with him wherever he went, just like Stone carried his pa. Staying might not help him fall out of love with Stone any quicker, but at least it would let him help Stone build the kind of stable, responsible, respectable life Stone seemed to want.

He glanced over at Jake, who was riding the fence with him that day. Stone had refused to let him go out alone since the blizzard; fortunately, Jake wasn't much of a talker, and so Luke didn't feel obliged to start up a conversation, instead retreating into his own thoughts once more.

As winter turned into spring, he'd been riding enough to break in the saddle Stone had given him for Christmas. He'd sold his old saddle to one of the hands and dutifully used the new one, not because he wanted to but because he didn't want to seem ungrateful. He understood what Stone had been trying to do, and he appreciated it. But even though it was indeed the finest thing he'd ever owned, he would have given away both the saddle and Mist in a heartbeat if it meant he could be with Stone. He took neither pride nor pleasure in the saddle, not when it represented the greatest loss of his entire life.

He was careful to avoid mentioning that Stone had given it to him as well, but for someone who was so damned worried about people talking, Stone was showing a considerable lack of discretion. Sometimes, Stone seemed hell-bent on treating Luke like his lover in every way short of sharing his bed. Luke had tried to remind him to be more careful. Giving Luke expensive presents and referring to "their ranch" and "their house" wasn't exactly going to make folks think Luke was nothing more than the foreman, especially since they hadn't known each other all that long. He thought maybe Stone understood what mixed messages he'd been sending to Luke and to everyone else, and he hoped Stone would back off and quit treating him like he was special. It was only making it harder for Luke's wounds to heal, and besides, if Stone was afraid of what would happen if people started talking about them, then he damned well needed to stop giving them reasons to talk in the first place.

Before he could continue down that depressing line of thought, he noticed cattle grazing in the distance outside where the Copper Lake ranch fence ought to be.

"Shit! Looks like we got ourselves a break," he said as he spurred Mist into a quicker pace. Jake kept up easily.

When they reached the far end of the pasture, he could see a fair bit of the fence had been torn down, as if the cattle had stampeded right over it, and he looked around to see how many remained inside the fenced area, dismayed by how few he saw milling around.

"How many head did we have out here?" he asked.

"About a hundred, I think," Jake replied. "Looks like most of them are gone."

"Well, let's see how many we can round up," Luke said grimly. "Maybe they ain't gone too far. We'll get them back inside the fence, and then I want you to get more men and supplies so we can get this fixed before nightfall."

"Mr. Harrison said I wasn't to leave you alone." Jake gave him a dubious look.

"Ain't no blizzard goin' to blow up today," Luke retorted, not bothering to hide his exasperation. "I'll be fine, and if I ain't, I'll take the blame so you won't have to."

They were only able to round up about twenty of the escaped cattle, and Luke began giving serious thought to suggesting Stone build up the horse-breeding angle, maybe even focus on breeding race horses. Beef prices weren't as good now as they had been a few years ago anyway, so it might be a good time to diversify.

Once they got as many cattle as they could find back inside the fence, Jake took off for the ranch, and Luke started repairing the fence, trying to salvage as much as possible. It wasn't long before he heard riders approaching, and he glanced up to see Jake had returned with a few hands and a wagon full of supplies. And Stone. For once, Luke was glad to see him; something wasn't sitting right about the damage he'd seen to the posts, and he wanted another pair of eyes on it.

"Looks like we lost eighty-some head or more," he said. "I reckon we could send some men out lookin' farther than Jake and I went, but I don't know how lucky we'll get in findin' them after this long."

Stone looked grim as he swung out of the saddle to look at the damage. "Damn." He glanced along the length of downed barbed wire and broken-off posts. "They must have been spooked. We'll have to move the rest of the herd into the lower pasture until we fix this."

Luke glanced at the other men, waiting until they were busy unloading the wagon, before pulling Stone aside. "I ain't so sure it was spooked cattle. Look at the marks on that post," he added, pointing to one of the broken posts on the ground. "Do they look funny to you?"

Stone frowned and crouched next to the fallen post, lifting up the broken end. He ran his finger along the crosswise part of the break, which was smooth along one side before becoming the normal, jagged spikes one expected from broken wood. "Sort of looks like it was cut part way, don't it?"

Luke nodded. "That's what I thought, but I wanted another opinion. Question is, if we're right, who would want to damage the fence? None of the other ranchers 'round here bear any grudges, so far as I know."

"Maybe rustlers who want to make it look like ain't nothin' been rustled." Stone dropped the post and moved to the next one, which looked the same. As he stood, Luke saw his expression was thunderous, and his brows were drawn together above eyes that held cold anger. "Cattle thieves think ranchers are stupid and lazy and won't look past the ends of their noses. Well, if they tried it once, they'll try it again. We need to send the men out to ride the fence and check for cuts elsewhere before we lose more cattle."

"Maybe we ought to set a regular patrol," Luke suggested. "Just in case they try again."

"Good idea." Stone nodded and looked at the hands, who were starting to unload new posts from the wagon. "Shorty! I want you to ride back and tell the rest of the hands to drop what they're doin'. Send four to move the cattle into the lower pasture, and the rest can start ridin' the fence line, looking for damage."

"Right, boss." Shorty touched the brim of his hat before mounting and heading off.

Stone turned back to Luke. "I need to tell the other ranchers in the area, too." He frowned again, as he thought of something. "Unless whoever did this was goin' after us in particular."

"I don't see why they would," Luke replied, shaking his head. "It must be rustlers, like you said."

"Yeah. Must be." Stone rubbed the back of his neck. "I guess I'm just feelin' put upon, after spendin' the mornin' with my 'cousin'." He rolled his eyes as he said the word. "Seems like he brought bad luck with him as well as *civilization*."

99

Luke tried to look properly sympathetic, but wasn't sure how well he managed it. He didn't envy Stone having to spend the whole morning with that annoying dandy, but he was very glad he had the excuse of work to get him out of the house.

"I don't suppose he said anything about the duration of his visit?"

"No, damn it." Stone looked disgusted. "I mentioned he might be more comfortable headin' back to Boston, but that man can't take a hint. He just said he rather liked roughin' it."

Luke grimaced, disheartened by that bad news. "It'd be a hell of a lot easier to put up with him if we knew when he was leavin'."

"Yeah. But the women in town don't feel the same way. You should have seen him smilin' at the ladies and kissin' hands like he was royalty. They ate it up with a spoon. The only good thing was he came away with enough dinner invites to last him two weeks."

"That's good!" Luke was willing to take any respite from Dandy Jim he could get, and if the ladies of Serenity could tolerate him better, well, Luke would be glad to chuck him in their midst without a qualm. "Maybe Mrs. Wilson'll latch onto him."

"Maybe, though I wouldn't wish that man on sweet little Agnes. 'Course, she's probably too smart to be taken in by his fancy talk." He pushed his hat back on his head. "Well, I guess we should get to work mendin' this fence. I'll leave it with you to set up patrols. If we need to hire more hands to cover it until fall, that's fine. We don't want to lose any more head before we can get them to market."

"No, we don't." Luke didn't like big losses, especially not preventable ones. "I'll get right on the patrol schedule. Remind me to tell you about an idea I had earlier," he added, deciding he would bring up the horse breeding idea after all. He had practice with tracking bloodlines; he'd been doing it informally for the horses born and bred on the ranch since Priss realized he had an interest in such things. "It might be time to think about movin' away from cattle."

Stone gave him a questioning look. "Is that so? I'll be interested in hearin' what that's all about. But let's talk about it away from the city slicker. That man is about as nosy as Mrs. Wilson."

"You won't get no argument out of me. I don't like the idea of him hearin' anything either," Luke agreed firmly. He wasn't sure why he distrusted James Rivers as well as disliked him, but he'd learned to depend on his instincts. "He ain't nothin' like Priss, that's for sure. I wouldn't take them for family if I didn't know different."

"They ain't blood kin, and I suppose he wasn't around her enough for good sense to rub off on him." Stone began to roll up his sleeves. "I don't know when I'll be back. I'm goin' to stay until we get this done."

Luke nodded and touched the brim of his hat. "Yes, sir. I'll make sure the men start patrollin' as soon as possible. If we need any extra hands, I'll have an estimate about how many ready for you when you get back."

He saw a flicker cross Stone's face at the "sir," but Stone simply nodded. "Right. And don't wait dinner. I don't want Dandy Jim to miss a meal and have cause to complain."

"I'll treat him as good as gold," Luke said dryly.

"Don't overdo it." Stone turned and headed to the wagon, lifting a large fence post out of the back by himself and carrying it over to where a couple of hands were working the broken end of a post out of the ground.

Luke couldn't help but watch, allowing himself the little luxury of admiring the display of strength and the play of muscles in Stone's arms. He felt a flare of heat in response to the sight, and he turned away and headed quickly back to Mist. There wasn't any point to looking when he couldn't touch, and he wasn't fool enough to torture himself over something he couldn't have.

15

STONE was dead tired by the time he accompanied the rest of the hands back to the stable, but he took time to care for Raider and thank his men for their hard work before dragging himself to the house. It was well after dark, so he wasn't surprised when he entered through the kitchen and found supper had already been cleaned up and put away.

He went to the sink and pumped the handle to set the water flowing, and then he dunked his head under it, gasping at the chill. Mary always left towels in reach, so he mopped himself up before going to the icebox to see what was left from supper.

"You're safe." Luke's voice came from behind him, startling him. "Dandy Jim went upstairs to take a bath. Apparently, he don't hold to our primitive ways, and he wants bath water heated up more'n once a week."

"That's a lot of bathin' for a man who don't look like he ever did a lick of work in his life," Stone replied. He pulled out a piece of ham and carried it over to the counter to make himself a sandwich. "We got the fence patched. Shorty said there didn't seem to be no more breaks."

"Good." Luke nodded, appearing satisfied with that news. "I got a patrol schedule written up and posted in the bunkhouse, and I went over it aloud, too, so those who can't read know when it's their turn to go out. If the rustlers try to hit the ranch again, we'll catch them right quick."

"Let's just hope they've moved on." Stone put his sandwich on a plate, poured a cup of coffee, and took a seat at the table with a weary sigh. "I'll need to go into town tomorrow and report to the sheriff, so he can be on the lookout. The cattle were branded, but rustlers ain't goin' to sell to anybody who cares about that. We'll have to write it off as a loss unless some miracle happens."

"Yeah." Luke sighed, and after a moment of visible hesitation, he sat down opposite Stone. "It may be time to cut back on sellin' cattle anyway. Beef prices have been droppin' the last few years, and it just ain't as profitable as it used to be."

Stone swallowed a bite of his sandwich and washed it down with coffee as he thought that over. "True enough. I even heard Mr. Stevenson sayin' last year he was worried about too many head on the market. So what is this idea you mentioned? But I warn you, if you say pig farmin', I'm goin' to pretend I didn't hear it."

Luke smiled a little at that, and he shook his head. "Nah, I ain't much interested in that myself. I was thinkin' more along the lines of breedin' horses. Folks need them for pullin' buggies and ridin', and racin's gettin' real popular, too."

"Horse breedin'?" Stone frowned in thought. Good horses did command a lot of money, but it took a lot more care in breeding and raising them than it did cattle, and you couldn't raise as many. "Well, it's a thought, but it's not like we could switch overnight. How could we breed enough to match what we make on beef, even if the price drops?"

"We don't have to give up cattle completely," Luke replied, seeming to grow more animated as he warmed up to the subject. "Just cut back so it ain't our only source of income. We could make a plan and breed more horses and less cattle over the next few years so the change ain't all sudden like. I've got bloodline records on the horses we already own. I've been in charge of the breedin' for a while," he added with obvious pride.

"Have you, now?" Stone was impressed with the work Luke had done. He'd known Priss had put an awful lot of trust in Luke, but apparently, she'd had even more confidence in him than he'd thought. "Was this somethin' you and Priss had been plannin' before she died?"

"Nah, it's just somethin' I've always had an interest in. She didn't mind me takin' over the breedin' for the ranch 'cause I knew what I was doin', and I got good results. Beef was sellin' so well, though, so we never talked about breedin' horses for more than just our own use. But that's how we got Mist and the rest of the grays."

Stone ate the rest of his sandwich as he mulled it over, weighing the pros and cons. He didn't know near enough about raising horses for market, but what Luke said made a lot of sense. If the price of beef fell a lot, they'd have something to fall back on other than just the mine, which didn't produce nearly enough to support the whole ranch and pay all the hands, plus the taxes.

"It seems like a good idea," he said. More than that, he'd not seen Luke so pleased about anything since their quarrel, and he couldn't bring himself to deny Luke something that made him happy and want to stay on the ranch. "Sure, go ahead and get started, so long as we don't have to lay out a lot of money right at the start. We're committed to the cattle this year, anyway, but we can see how much we make when we go to market and then figure out what to do by the time winter comes. And we'll talk about how much more land we'd have to turn over to hayin'. That suit?"

"Yes, sir." Luke's smile widened, and an anticipatory light appeared in his eyes, as if he was already making plans.

Stone suppressed a sigh as Luke called him "sir" again, and he rose from the table to take his cup and plate to the sink. He was glad to have made Luke happy, but he knew there probably wasn't anything he could do that would bring back the easy, carefree Luke he'd first met, and that gave him a pang every time he thought about it.

A loud clatter followed by a crash from outside startled Stone out of his morose train of thought.

"What in the hell?" Stone turned and ran for the door, yanking it open and jumping down the stairs as he ran in the direction of the noise.

Luke followed close on his heels, looking around wildly for the source. There were shouts from the bunkhouse as well, and several of the hands ran out, holding lanterns.

"Over here!" Stone heard the shout from behind the stable, and he veered in that direction, skidding to a halt and staring in dismay as the lanterns revealed what had happened.

A twisted mass of broken wood and metal lay at the foot of the windmill, where the bladed head had come off and crashed to the ground below. Stone stared at this fresh catastrophe in disbelief. "Now how in the hell did that happen?"

"Maybe somethin' came loose." Luke looked down at the wreckage with growing dismay. "Oh *hell*, this is goin' to be expensive."

"I take it we don't have an extra one in the barn."

Luke shook his head somberly, his expression letting Stone know exactly how serious the situation was. "No, we can't even get a replacement in town. We'll have to send someone to Reno."

"Damn." Stone wanted to grind his teeth in frustration. The last few days had been bad, and he hoped there were no more nasty surprises waiting to jump out at him. The hands were subdued, and he knew he had to act decisively to keep their spirits up, since they knew the fortunes of the ranch could affect their livelihood. "Well, I guess that means someone's gettin' a free trip to Reno." He looked at the assembled men and made a quick decision, choosing two of the hands he knew could be trusted to resist the urge to drink and carouse. "Brent, Dave, I want you to take the buckboard and head to Reno tomorrow mornin'. You'll need to stay the night, but I need you back the day after with that blade head."

"Yes, boss," Dave acknowledged, and Stone nodded, knowing he would do as he was told.

Stone looked at Luke. "Do you need to go with 'em? I almost hate to let you do it, just in case any other disasters crop up here. I can't be in two places at once."

"I probably should," Luke replied. "I know what to get, and it'll be easier for me to pay for it if we need to use credit at the bank."

"Right." Stone raked his fingers through his hair. "Well, no sense worryin' about this mess tonight. In the mornin', before you go, we'll check to make sure nothin' in the gearbox was damaged," He gave Luke a sour look. "If I were a suspicious man, I'd say you were goin' just to get away from Dandy Jim for a couple of days."

"The thought hadn't even crossed my mind," Luke said dryly.

"Sure it didn't." Stone gave him a dubious look, and then raised his voice. "Okay, everyone go on back inside. We had a hard day today, and looks like everyone'll need their rest for tomorrow."

With that, he turned and headed back toward the house. He was beginning to understand why some of the ranchers he'd worked for had looked old before their time.

16

AFTER the problems of the past couple of days, Luke counted himself lucky indeed that nothing went wrong on the trip to Reno. They didn't get waylaid, the part was available, and neither Brent nor Dave made fools of themselves. Well, not fools enough that Luke had to bail them out of jail, at least. He let them have a night out, but he remained at the hotel; he didn't much care what kind of entertainments the big city offered, and he didn't want to put a damper on Dave and Brent's good time.

The part was expensive enough, but Priss had set the example of always putting aside funds for emergencies, and Luke reckoned this counted as such. He was glad he'd carried on her habit and convinced Stone it was a good idea as well, because they'd already lost cattle, and it was just the beginning of the season; there would be more inevitable losses from disease and predators before the market.

In hindsight, he supposed he ought to have known *something* would happen the way their luck had been running at the ranch lately, and he felt a growing sense of foreboding as he regarded the somber faces of the men clustered just outside the barn as he, Dave, and Brent rode up. He dismounted quickly and handed Mist's reins to the nearest stable hand, and he approached Shorty, dreading whatever bad news he was about to hear.

"What happened? Did more cattle get out?"

"If only that was it!" Shorty turned to Luke, and Luke could see the anxiety in his eyes. "It's Mr. Harrison. We was goin' to ride out to the mine to check on the shipment due to go out, and when he went to mount Raider, that horse went plumb crazy. Mr. Harrison only had one foot in the stirrups, and Raider reared back and threw him. It weren't Raider's fault, neither, because I found a burr under his blanket when I unsaddled him." Burrs were a fact of life, and one under the saddle could cause a horse a lot of pain. Shorty shook his head and swallowed hard. "It looked like a bad fall. We got him in the house, and Charlie rode to fetch Doc Wilson. The doc's inside now, but he told us to wait out here. Can you find out what's happenin', Luke? We're all worried."

Luke felt like all of his insides were frozen, and he swallowed hard, trying not to let his rising panic show in front of the hands. For all his grumbling about Stone revealing too much, he was on the verge of doing the same thing, and he couldn't afford that luxury. Instead, he nodded, trying to appear calm and reassuring for the men.

"I'll do that." He patted Shorty's shoulder. And he meant it. No one was going to stand in the way of him finding out what had happened and more importantly, if Stone was all right.

His jaw set, he strode toward the big house and went inside, heading straight for the stairs. No doubt they'd taken Stone up to his bedroom, and Luke took the steps two at a time. The bedroom door was open, and Luke stopped on the threshold, peering inside anxiously.

"What's goin' on, Doc?" he asked in a hushed voice.

Doc Wilson was a solid, gray-haired man who'd birthed or buried many of the folks in Serenity. He glanced back over his shoulder and grunted when he recognized Luke. He was blocking Luke's view of the bed, but he moved aside and beckoned Luke to come in.

Stone was lying beneath a sheet, looking paler than Luke had ever seen him. There was a bandage wrapped around his head and another around his bare chest. His eyes were closed, and he seemed to be breathing more shallowly than Luke thought proper.

"He's mighty lucky," the doctor said, keeping his voice low. "I got him on laudanum right now to keep him still and dull the pain. He's cracked a couple of ribs, but lucky for him, he's got a head as hard as his name. That fall rang his bell pretty good, but I don't think he's broken his skull or scrambled his brains overmuch."

Luke swallowed hard, relieved the news hadn't been worse. "Mary and me will take care of him. What do we need to do?"

"Keep him still, if he'll stay still," the doctor replied sourly. "That one's got a powerful strong will. I'll leave you some laudanum to dose him with if he's hurting or if he gives you too much sass. If he doesn't start vomiting blood, he'll be all right in a couple of weeks. Ah, there you are, Aggie. You've got those extra bandages I sent you for?"

"Yes, Papa." Agnes Wilson stepped into the room, smiling kindly at Luke before handing her father a stack of neatly rolled white linen. Luke welcomed her presence, because she seemed to radiate an air of quiet competence he found soothing. "I told Mama you wouldn't be too late for supper."

"Thanks, darlin'," the doctor replied as he piled the bandages on the table next to Stone's bed. He turned back to Luke. "You've seen cracked ribs before, I'm sure. You need to keep him wrapped up tight so he doesn't break what's only bruised right now."

"I'll make sure he don't. He'll be still, Doc. I'll see to it, even if me'n the boys have to hitch him to the bedposts. How long before he can get up at all? I'm sure that'll be the first question he'll ask, but I ain't about to let him up no sooner."

"He can get up in the morning, if he's feeling like it. No work, though." Doc Wilson pulled a bottle out of his bag and handed it to Luke. "The dose is written on the label. Don't let him drink any alcohol while he's taking that." He closed his bag and rested his hand on Luke's shoulder. "He'll be all right. I know you don't want to think about the ranch getting another new owner now you're getting this one broken in. Tell the boys not to worry. He'll be back to ordering them around in no time."

109

Privately, Luke thought it might not hurt to tell Stone he'd been confined to bed rest for at least a couple of days just to be on the safe side, but he nodded an acknowledgment of Doc Wilson's instructions.

"You're right." Luke mustered a smile. "I just about got him trained right, and I ain't ready to take on anyone new, so I'll take good care of him. He'll follow your instructions. I'll see to it myself."

"Good man. Well, I'd best be off. Aggie girl, let's leave Luke to it." With that, the doctor nodded to Luke and headed out the door.

Agnes paused on her way out and patted his arm. "He'll be all right," she said softly, her brown eyes full of sympathy. "Papa would have told you if it was worse. It might be best to have someone sit with him at night, though, in case he tries to get up." She paused, hesitating for a moment before continuing. "He was asking for you before he fell asleep. Luke, be careful who sits with him, all right? Laudanum can cause people to say some interesting things."

Luke peered at her searchingly, wondering what she might have already heard or guessed but afraid to ask. Instead, he kept his expression as neutral as possible and simply nodded. "I'll surely keep that in mind, Miss Agnes. Thanks for lettin' me know."

"Of course, Luke." She smiled at him warmly. "I'll have a talk with Mary before we go. She should know just how crazy people can talk sometimes when they're dosed. I want to make sure she knows it doesn't mean anything at all." With that she left the room, the faint scent of lemon verbena trailing behind her.

Luke silently groaned at the indirect confirmation that Stone had said *something* to make her suspect the truth. For a moment, he was tempted to run after her and ask what it was so he'd know what he was fighting against, but since she seemed willing either to ignore it or help explain it away, he decided he was better off not knowing. He was getting damned tired of having all the problems of a secret relationship without any of the benefits that would make having to hide more tolerable.

He moved to stand beside Stone's bed. "Figures," he said, shaking his head at Stone even though a scolding would do no good now. "Any other time, you won't say 'peas' for a potful, but you get a drop of laudanum in you, and suddenly, you want to tell the whole world your secrets. Well, you can be damned sure I ain't lettin' anyone else stay with you while you're takin' it."

There was a plain wooden chair by the window, and Luke dragged it over to the bed and sat down, folding his arms across his chest.

"And you can forget about gettin' out of that bed tomorrow too," he added with a stubborn frown.

He watched Stone's silent form, carefully monitoring the rise and fall of Stone's chest. It was easy enough to set down his rules, especially when Stone wasn't awake to hear them, but he knew the battle would begin once Stone woke up. Luke had doctor's orders on his side, and he intended to make sure Stone got plenty of rest and healed up proper, whether Stone liked it or not.

It wasn't long before Mary came up to see if there was anything she could do, and Luke sent her to tell Shorty and the rest of the hands Stone would be confined to bed for a few days, but he would be fine. He also requested a few newspapers to keep him occupied while he kept vigil beside Stone's bed, and he settled in as comfortably as the wood chair allowed to watch and wait.

By the time he finished up the last newspaper Mary had brought, afternoon was turning into evening, and when he heard footsteps on the stairs, he thought maybe Mary was bringing his supper.

Unfortunately, however, it was the last person he wanted to see. James swept into the room and stared at Stone's unconscious form with a shock that somehow didn't seem quite believable.

"Why, whatever happened? I go into town for a few hours, and suddenly everything goes wrong."

Because losin' cattle and an important piece of equipment takin' damage don't qualify as things "goin' wrong," Luke thought sourly, but he didn't say that aloud as he struggled to remain polite. "Stone got thrown. Doc's been out. He'll be fine in a few days."

"My poor cousin." James shook his head and sighed. "It seems ranching is a terribly dangerous business, doesn't it? He didn't crack his skull open, did he?" James peered at the bandage around Stone's head and shivered theatrically. "I hate the sight of blood."

Luke offered a tight smile. "Your concern for your cousin is mighty touchin'. But don't you worry none. He's hard-headed in more ways'n one."

James's blue eyes narrowed as he frowned down at Luke. "I don't appreciate being talked to in that tone of voice by the *help*," he snapped, sounding annoyed and not at all conciliatory, as he always seemed to be in Stone's presence. "My cousin's plebeian origins obviously prompt him to treat his employees as though they were friends, but you need to remember who your betters are."

Luke knew he ought to "stay in his place" for Stone's sake, especially since they had no idea how long James intended to remain, and he had *tried* to behave, showing proper deference to Stone in James' presence. Men like James Rivers didn't intimidate him, and while he wanted to make Stone look good in James's eyes, as well as avoid making people talk, a man had his limits, and Luke had just about reached his. Too much had happened in the past few days, and he'd come home to find the man he loved laid up with cracked ribs. He was in no mood to act deferential tonight.

Looking James in the eye, he replied, "I do remember."

He had the satisfaction of seeing James turn scarlet, and for a moment, he thought James might lunge at him across the bed. But then James seemed to get himself under control, although he didn't bother to mask his dislike as he peered at Luke down the length of his nose. "I won't forget this," he bit out. "You can rest assured of that."

He didn't wait for Luke to reply before storming out of the room and down the hall. Luke heard the door to the front room slam, and then everything was silent.

Aw, hell, Luke silently groaned. He should have kept his mouth shut and continued the pretense of respect, but he'd let his temper get the better of him. There was no telling what kind of trouble he'd stirred up for Stone, but maybe it wouldn't be too bad. If they were really lucky, James might pack up his bags and head back to the big city that much sooner.

It was a long shot, he knew, but a man could dream.

17

WAKING up was a matter of leaving dark, disturbing dreams for a brighter but painful reality. Stone opened his eyes slowly and drew in a deep breath that caused him to gasp in pain. "Shit," he ground out as he tried to sit up.

"Oh no, you don't!" The response was immediate, startling him, and then Luke was looming over him, pressing his shoulders back down. "You're to lie still."

"Luke?" Stone stared up at the man he loved and smiled. Luke was there, and suddenly things seemed a lot better. "When did you get home?"

"A few hours ago." Luke sat down again, regarding him sternly. "And a fine welcome home I got, too, findin' out you couldn't stay on a horse's back worth a damn."

Stone frowned, trying to remember what had happened despite the muddled feeling in his head, and slowly the pieces came back. He'd started to mount Raider, and the next thing he knew, he was looking up at Doc Wilson, who was asking him what day it was.

"Raider threw me," he said, the thought disturbing him deeply. "He's never done that before."

"He had a burr under his blanket." Luke smiled crookedly. "You must have been mighty distracted to miss that. You should be more careful."

"I thought I checked." Stone tried to focus his thoughts, which seemed to be scattered all over the place. "I guess I was thinkin' about the windmill."

"I reckon so. It can happen to anyone." Luke gave him another stern look. "Just don't let it happen again."

"I'll sure try." Stone shook his head and quickly decided that was a bad idea. He lifted his hand to his temple, surprised to find he was all wrapped up. "How bad am I hurt?"

"Could be worse," Luke replied gruffly, tugging up the light blanket covering Stone and smoothing it. "Cracked ribs and a bump on the head. You've got to be still so those cracked ribs don't turn into busted ribs."

Stone frowned at the mere thought of staying in bed much longer. "I can't do that, and you know it." His head was slowly clearing, and he remembered why Luke had gone away in the first place. "You get that part?"

"The hell you can't stay in that bed!" Luke rounded on him with a scowl. "Yeah, I got the part, and it's goin' to get installed, and this ranch is goin' to do just fine without you stompin' around it for a few days."

"But...." Stone stared at Luke, and the sight of Luke's lips turned down made Stone forget what he'd been about to say. Luke was too handsome to wear a frown like that. "I like it better when you smile."

Luke froze, his expression shifting from irate to shocked, and he gaped at Stone in silence before he recovered enough to speak. "Well, when I have reason to, I'll smile," he said. "Meanwhile, you're goin' to behave yourself and rest like Doc Wilson said to."

Stone was torn. He didn't want to stay in bed, but he didn't want to make Luke unhappy either. He'd already caused Luke too much pain as it was; that was why Luke rarely smiled anymore, and he knew it. "Sorry. I didn't mean to cause you so much trouble. Why ain't anything ever easy?"

"I don't know. It's just how life is, I reckon," Luke replied quietly, turning his gaze to the wood floor. "You find a way through the rough patches and keep goin' as best you can."

"Been tryin'. Just want a few less rough patches, is all." Stone sighed. "'Least I can count on you."

"Yeah, you can." Luke fluffed Stone's pillow a little. "And right now, you can count on me to make sure you get the rest you need until Doc Wilson says your ribs are okay."

Stone peered at Luke, and then he reached out to capture Luke's hand. "You can count on me too, y'know."

"I know." Luke let his hand remain in Stone's for a moment longer before tugging it free.

"Good." Stone smiled, relieved Luke understood. He was suddenly feeling tired again, and he closed his eyes and sighed. "Guess I need a little rest. Just don't let me sleep too long, okay?"

"You sleep as long as you need to. The ranch'll be fine, and I ain't goin' nowhere."

"Good." Luke's words were reassuring, and Stone let himself relax. Somehow, everything would be just fine, so long as Luke was there. "This is where you belong," he murmured, and then he felt himself slipping back into darkness once again.

18

THE little town of Serenity could look right festive when it wanted to, Luke thought as he walked along Main Street, which was illuminated by lanterns hung on shepherd's hooks that were decorated with fresh greenery and flowers in honor of the Spring Festival. What had begun as a simple town picnic to celebrate the arrival of spring a couple of years before Luke's arrival had evolved into a day-long festival with games, fireworks, and a dance on top of the traditional picnic lunch. After the recent run of bad luck on the ranch, Luke was glad for a reason to forget all the losses and expenses for a while, even if he didn't feel much like celebrating, and it was nice to see folks laughing and having a good time.

Now that the sun had set and the fireworks were over, children were being taken home to bed, some of them already exhausted enough to fall asleep in their pa's arms and some of them kicking up a fuss. But the day had been full of events aimed at entertaining the little ones, and now it was the adults' turn to have some fun at the dance. Luke could already hear the band warming up as he approached the warehouse that had been cleaned up and cleared out for the occasion.

He saw Stone hovering near the entrance, and he mustered as much of a smile as he could. He'd managed to keep himself occupied with activities that put some distance between himself and Stone, needing to forget *that* situation for a little while too. Stone had recuperated from being thrown quickly, which was a blessing for Luke's nerves; it had taken everything in him to keep from fussing and hovering like a mother hen while Stone rested and healed, but that wouldn't have done either of them any good in the long run.

He had no doubt Stone was unsettled by the thought of attending the dance, which meant Stone needed him for reassurance, moral support, and help in escaping unwanted entanglements. Going to church every week was one thing; they could be in and out the door quickly enough to not get dragged into a lot of socializing, but here, the mixing and mingling couldn't be avoided, and there would be hopeful young ladies fishing for invitations to dance from both of them. Luke didn't mind that so much; he had always danced with the eligible misses and some of the matrons as well, giving the ladies enough attention to appear sociable, but not giving any of them concrete reason to hope they had caught his eye.

"I hope you ain't thinkin' about runnin' off," he said as he approached Stone. "You should stay a little while, at least."

Stone shifted uncomfortably and shrugged. Luke could see that he was trying hard to look as though he wasn't as nervous as Luke was sure he was feeling. He was in a new suit, too, a dark blue one with a white shirt that made his skin look very tanned.

"I reckon I'll have to," he muttered. "Since it's *proper* Copper Lake Ranch be represented." He gave Luke a slightly sour look, because the only reason Stone had agreed to come in the first place was that Luke had pointed out Priss would have expected it of him. For all that Stone had never known his aunt, he seemed determined to hold to things the same way she would have done them, and Luke had found that saying "Priss would've…." was a good way to get Stone to cave in on things when he was being particularly stubborn.

"Well, it is." Luke didn't feel a trace of guilt about using any weapon in his arsenal he had to. "Priss never missed the Spring Festival, and she always attended the dance, even though she couldn't dance with the one she really wanted to dance with."

As soon as the words were out of his mouth, Luke regretted saying them because all he'd managed to do was remind himself he was in the exact same situation Priss had been in all those years. It definitely didn't put him in a festive mood.

Apparently it didn't do much for Stone, either, since he sighed and looked away. "I ain't dancin'. If I've got to say my ribs are worse than they are, I will. But I don't want to take a chance of steppin' on some dainty gal's toes. Not to mention havin' to *talk*."

"Fine, you can stand around with the married men and jaw about cattle," Luke replied soothingly. "I'll do the dancin'."

Stone's eyes were back on him at once, dark and intense. "You will?" His jaw worked as though he wanted to say something else, but then he shrugged again. "I guess that makes sense."

"I don't mind it." Luke mirrored his shrug. It wasn't what he wanted to do, but it was the right thing to do, especially since it would maintain the illusion that he was no different from any other man in his preferences. "I do it every year."

"Well, maybe you'll catch a break this year." Stone inclined his head toward the wall where James was currently holding court with half a dozen of the town girls hanging on his every word. "Looks like ol' Dandy Jim might be the belle of this particular ball."

"Figures." Luke didn't bother to hide his disgust. He wasn't particularly upset that James would be relieving him of the burden of socializing with the unmarried young ladies of Serenity, but he had no doubt James would be as phony and smarmy with the ladies as he had been with everyone at Copper Lake, and that sat wrong with Luke. At least he didn't lead the girls on, but he doubted James would draw the same line. "Well, as long as he behaves, I don't much mind having my dancing duties lightened."

"Him behavin' is the big question, ain't it?" Stone's eyes narrowed as he looked at his cousin. "Maybe I was selfish, bein' glad he was leavin' me alone to recover. Seems like he might have been settlin' himself in to stay for a long spell."

"Unfortunately," Luke agreed grimly. He hadn't mentioned his confrontation with James to Stone. For one thing, he was annoyed with himself for letting James provoke him to rudeness, and for another, he didn't want Stone to worry. While Luke was sure James hadn't forgotten it any more than he had, they seemed to have reached an unspoken agreement to ignore what had happened.

"I just wish I knew what'd convince him to go back East," Stone said, gnawing on his bottom lip. "I wish I knew the *real* reason he was here."

"Me too." Luke drew in a deep breath and braced himself for an evening of socializing that for once, he wasn't in the mood for. "Well, time to get started, I reckon." He stepped inside the warehouse and headed straight for the refreshment table. The punch wouldn't be spiked, unfortunately, but eating and drinking would at least give him something to do that would let him procrastinate on the socializing.

Agnes Wilson was standing behind the table, and she smiled as he approached. "Something to drink, Luke? We have lemonade. Papa had the lemons sent all the way from San Francisco just for the Festival."

"Really?" Luke was genuinely impressed by that, and he didn't try to hide it, knowing it would please Agnes. "In that case, I'd love some."

Agnes's smile widened, and she picked up one of the mugs on the table, filling it carefully with a ladle from a huge bowl of the lemonade. "There you are." She hesitated for a moment. "How is Mr. Harrison doing?"

"Back to his normal ornery self." Luke gave her a mischievous smile. "He was up as soon as possible and back to work. Your pa did a good job patchin' him up."

"Papa is a good doctor." She didn't bother to hide the pride she felt in her father, but then her expression fell a little. "I would have liked to have been a doctor or at least a nurse, but Mama doesn't think it's ladylike. So instead I help Papa because that way, he doesn't have to pay a real nurse." She smiled slightly. "At least it gets me out of the house so I don't have to sit around doing the fancy embroidery Mama thinks will catch me a proper husband."

"I don't know of any man who'd care much about needlework, but he'd definitely appreciate someone who could take care of him when he ain't feelin' good." Luke didn't really know what men looked for in a woman, but he could take a decent guess.

Agnes chuckled, and her brown eyes sparkled, making her look almost pretty. "You're right, but my Mama does cling to what her own mama taught her. At least she finally listened when I told her Mr. Harrison could never, ever be interested in me."

Luke schooled his features into a neutral expression, not wanting to give away too much. This wasn't the first time Agnes had said something that hinted at her knowing more than she ought to, but Luke would be damned if he would confirm anything for her. Not when Stone refused to be with him out of fear of what people might think if they found out.

"Well, now, Miss Agnes, you never know who might take a fancy to you."

She shook her head, her cheeks turning pink. "Oh no, though you're nice to say it, Luke." Her gaze moved to where James was laughing and joking with what seemed to be every single woman under thirty in town—with the exception of Agnes. "People get so wrapped up in what a woman looks like, they don't see anything else."

Luke let out a disgusted snort at James' posing and preening. "You deserve a lot better than anything that fancy fool has to offer," he said, and he meant it. Agnes might have a plain face, but she was smart and had a good heart, and James Rivers was the last man who could make her happy.

Unfortunately, it seemed his encouragement may have come too late. Agnes shook her head, looking down into the bowl of lemonade. "It doesn't matter. Remember how I told you I'd know when the right man came along? Only he isn't the right one. He's just the one I want, even though I thought I was too smart to fall for a handsome face." She lifted her eyes to Luke again, and there was a kind of empathy in them mixed with sadness. "Love isn't easy, is it? At least not for some of us."

"I ain't so sure it's easy for any of us," he replied, refusing to give in to the urge to look at Stone. He wasn't about to be stupid and give himself away like that. He regarded her speculatively for a moment and then put his cup aside; it seemed she was in as much need of a distraction as he was, and he knew one thing that might help. "Sounds like the band's startin' up a new tune," he said, beckoning to her. "Would you do me the honor, Miss Agnes?"

Her eyes widened, and she straightened her shoulders and curtseyed. "Mr. Reynolds, I would be delighted to dance with you." She came around the table and rested her hand on his arm, carrying herself with all the regal hauteur of a queen.

Luke escorted her over to the rest of the dancers, ignoring the gawking and whispering that followed in their wake, and led her smoothly and gracefully through the opening steps of a reel. Agnes was a very good dancer, even though Luke suspected her father had probably partnered her more than any of the single men in town, and Luke liked to dance, especially with a skilled partner. Even though he spotted Stone and James watching them intently, he ignored them, focusing his attention on Agnes. He was going to enjoy this, damn it, and make sure she did, too, since it might be the highlight of the evening for both of them.

When the reel ended, Agnes smiled breathlessly at him. "Thank you so much. That was fun!" Her cheeks were pink, and little wisps of brown hair had escaped from the tight bun she wore it in. "But I should get back to the refreshment table before the lemonade runs dry."

"Now, you wouldn't do that and leave me standing here in the middle of the floor by myself, would you, dear lady?"

Luke turned, but he recognized that voice, and he knew exactly who he'd see. Sure enough, James Rivers had decided to grace them with his presence, although he ignored Luke completely and focused his attention on Agnes, who was staring at him, wide-eyed. James seemed to take that as his due, however, and clasped her unresisting hand, lifting it to his lips as he bent over it. "Miss Agnes, you would break my heart if you didn't agree to dance with me."

Normally so self-possessed, Agnes looked like a rabbit caught in a coyote's sight. Then she nodded as though she were in a daze. "Of course, Mr. Rivers. I'd be honored to dance with you."

Luke scowled at James, knowing the man was up to *something*. He just didn't know what it was, but there would damned sure be hell to pay if James broke Agnes's heart on purpose. He didn't have any grounds to interfere, however, and there was no doubt Agnes wanted to dance with James. So Luke smiled at her and murmured his thanks for the dance, and then he retreated to fetch his cup from the refreshment table.

Stone was already there, and he was scowling again. "Now what's he doin'?" he muttered. "I swear, he only asked her to dance because you did first. Before that, he wasn't payin' her no mind at all."

Luke nodded as the pieces fell into place. "That's exactly what he did," he replied, taking a sip of lemonade, which was indeed quite good. "He probably thought he was showin' me up by takin' away the girl he thinks I'm interested in."

Stone frowned again. "Shows how much he knows. He'd best not hurt her. She's worth ten of him."

"Damned right she is." Luke glared at James's back, for all the good it did. Agnes looked like she was in heaven, and he couldn't begrudge her that. At least one of them would have a moment to remember that night.

"I don't know whether I should have a talk with him or not." He looked off to the side and shook his head. "Mrs. Wilson looks like she's ready to start sendin' out weddin' invitations any moment." Indeed, the Wilson matriarch was standing with her hands clasped to her bosom and watching her daughter and James as though wedding bells were ringing in her head.

"Somehow, I doubt he's got such honorable intentions," Luke replied grimly. "I'll keep an eye on him and make sure he don't take advantage of her."

"You and me both."

Before Luke could say anything else, Nelson Simmons walked past. Nelson was a grizzled, fifty-something rancher who owned a spread south of town, and he nodded to Luke, but when Stone greeted him politely, he scowled.

"Was a time when your kind weren't allowed among civilized folk," he snarled as he brushed by, heading toward the door.

"Wait just a danged minute!" Luke checked his language just in time, out of deference to the mixed company, and strode forward and grabbed Nelson's arm. "What the devil are you talkin' about?"

The older man shrugged off Luke's hand. "Your boss," he snapped, looking over at Stone, who was standing, still as a statue, staring at them. "Don't tell me you didn't know he was part Injun, Luke. His kind ain't nothin' but a bunch of savages."

"Yeah, I know what he is, and I don't care." Luke was furious, a surge of white-hot anger sweeping over him at Nelson's narrow-minded blathering. "My boss ain't no savage, and I don't reckon his kind has done any more murderin' than our kind has."

"You can say that. You didn't lose your Pa to a maraudin' band of Sioux!" Nelson's hands were clenched at his sides. "And I sure as hell don't have to stay in the same room with him, boy, or do business with him if I don't want to."

"No, you don't have to do none of that, but you better not let me hear you talkin' about him like that again." Luke lifted his chin defiantly. "Or you'll answer to me. Mr. Harrison is a good rancher and a good businessman, and Mrs. Harrison wanted him to have Copper Lake. That's all anyone needs to know."

Nelson's eyes narrowed. "Ain't your place to tell me what I can or can't say. I notice you ain't callin' me a liar. I'll talk about the truth all I want, and ain't nobody goin' to stop me!"

The band had stopped playing, and everything had gone quiet. In that silence, Stone spoke up, his deep voice soft but easy to hear.

"My mama was half Pawnee. Her pa was a white teacher, and her ma was the daughter of a medicine man. There weren't a more lovin', gentle person than my ma, and she weren't no savage." He was staring at Nelson, his face as hard as Luke had ever seen it. "You can say what you want about me, Mr. Simmons, but the truth of the matter is my pa was the savage. He got blind drunk and beat his wife and child for no reason other than meanness. And he was a white man."

Luke knew from what little Stone had said about his pa the man had been a no-account dog, but he hadn't realized Stone had been abused as well. Stone's desperation to prove he was nothing like his pa made even more sense now, and it explained why Stone had so many ghosts trailing after him.

He could think of nothing to say, and so he stared challengingly at Nelson instead, daring the man to offer more insults. If Nelson had any sense, he'd shut his mouth, but Luke wasn't sure just how much sense the man had.

Before he had to find out, Sheriff Anderson stepped between them. "I reckon that's enough name callin' and bad feelin's for now." Nelson opened his mouth, but the Sheriff glared at him. "Don't make me start tossin' folks in jail for disruptin' a public event. Your missus is home sick, as I recall. I don't think she'd be too happy about havin' to get out of bed to pay your bail, do you?"

Nelson snapped his mouth closed, glared at everyone, and then he turned on his heel and stomped out. Once he was gone, Sheriff Anderson smiled at the remaining crowd. "Well, then, since Nelson is bein' so reasonable, I think the rest of us can go on, don't you?"

The band started to play again, but no one seemed to feel like dancing. People did mill around, however, and when Luke glanced over to where Stone had been, all he got was a glimpse of his back as he headed toward the back door, people parting silently to let him through. Luke didn't hesitate to go after him, hurrying to catch up.

"Not everyone thinks like Nelson," he said. "I sure as hell don't."

Stone stopped and turned, the darkness making his features difficult to read. "I know you don't." His voice was rough. "But he won't be the only one who does. I don't care so much for me, but I have to think about the ranch. If me ownin' it is goin' to wreck everything Priss worked for, maybe I should think about sellin' it."

Luke shook his head vehemently, and he wasn't thinking about himself, but of Stone. Running the ranch had given Stone a chance to settle down and take on responsibility, and it had done him a world of good already. Stone needed a purpose and a way to assure himself he was nothing like his pa, and giving up the ranch would undermine all the confidence he'd built up over the last few months.

"Priss knew about your mama," Luke reminded him. "She left the ranch to you anyway. She wanted *you* to have it, and you're doin' good. You shouldn't give it up just because some fools judge you for who begot you. They ain't worth it, and there's plenty of reasonable folks who'll be glad to do business with you."

He could feel the weight of Stone's gaze on him. "I don't know. Maybe, but maybe not. Maybe Priss chose the wrong man. She should've given the ranch to you."

"I ain't her kin." Luke waved the thought away dismissively. "I got no claim to it, and I don't want none. I know what I'm good at, and that's bein' the foreman. I ain't got no desire to be the man in charge."

Stone was silent for a long moment, as though considering Luke's words. "But you were her friend. That gives you a better claim than a stranger, blood kin or not." Stone raked his hand through his hair. "You know what bugs me, though? Why now? I've been here almost six months, and ain't no one said a word about my folks. So far as I know, the only person who knows about my ma is you."

"Well, I reckon some folks have guessed," Luke pointed out. "You don't look all that white. But it *is* odd that no one's said anything about it before."

"I'm startin' to feel right put upon." Stone grimaced and straightened his shoulders. "But I suppose there's nothin' to do except go back in there and keep my chin up. People'll just talk more if I run off with my tail between my legs."

"You're right about that," Luke acknowledged, nodding somberly. It might not be easy, but at least if Stone returned to the dance with his head held high, he would show everyone he had nothing to hide or be ashamed of. "I'll stay close by, if you want me to."

Stone gave him a rather lopsided smile. "I'd be mighty grateful if you did. And thank you, for defendin' me. Ain't nobody ever stood up for me like that before."

Luke shrugged awkwardly and looked away; he hadn't thought twice before confronting Nelson, and he hoped he hadn't given away more than he ought to about how he felt. "No need to thank me for doin' what's right. You don't deserve that kind of disrespect, and I ain't goin' to listen to it if it comes from the president's own mouth."

"Well, I do appreciate it anyway," Stone replied. "Come on, let's get back inside." He headed back toward the building with grim determination. No doubt Stone wasn't going to enjoy the rest of the evening one bit, but having the toughness to stick it out was going to earn him respect from some people.

19

"THAT'LL be twelve dollars and fifty-six cents, Mr. Harrison. You want me to put it on the ranch account?"

"I'd be obliged if you did, Mr. Stephens." Stone nodded to the storekeeper as he picked up two twenty-five pound sacks of flour from the counter, hefting them in his arms and giving a slight grimace. It had been nearly three weeks since Raider had thrown him, but he still got a twinge from time to time.

"You want me to take that, Stone?" Little Sam was looking at him anxiously, but Stone shook his head.

"You get those bags of beans and potatoes and the spices Mary wanted." He jerked his chin toward Mr. Stephens and headed out the door. The buckboard was tethered in front of Stephen's Mercantile, and Stone put the flour sacks in the back, glad the chore of shopping was nearly finished and he and Little Sam could head back to the ranch.

Pushing his hat back on his head, he glanced down Serenity's Main Street as Little Sam loaded the rest of the supplies. One or two people pointedly ignored him as they passed by, but everyone else nodded to him politely. Despite his worries the night of the Spring Festival, only a few of the townsfolk seemed to find him socially unacceptable, and none of those were people he particularly liked anyway. They could snub him in church or in the street, but when it came down to it, Stone realized he'd found more acceptance in Serenity than he'd ever imagined possible. Most folk didn't seem to care who his mother had been; Priss had wanted him to have the ranch, and he was running it in a way she would have approved of, so that was good enough for them.

"That's the last of it." Little Sam grinned as he shut the gate on the back of the wagon. "We'll be home in time for supper."

"Always thinkin' about your stomach." Stone hauled himself up onto the seat and took the reins. Once Little Sam was seated next to him, Stone clucked to the horses and started them off on the journey home.

Little Sam pulled out a piece of taffy wrapped in wax paper from his pocket, unwrapped it, and popped it into his mouth. Stone shook his head, and Little Sam chuckled, settling back on the seat and happily chewing his sweet.

Stone turned his attention to the road, although there really wasn't much to see once they got out of town except for grass and the mountains they were headed toward. The horses knew the way, so Stone found himself thinking, as he often did, about Luke.

Luke's defense of him in front of the whole town had surprised him, and while he'd secretly been touched and pleased by it, he'd also worried anyone with two eyes in their head would see what was between him and Luke. After Luke had accused him of acting like a protective lover, the last thing Stone had expected was for Luke to turn around and do the same thing.

The next day, he'd overheard Luke dressing down one of the hands. He hadn't heard what the man said, but he arrived at the stables just in time to catch Luke's raised voice. "You'll do your job with a smile on your lips and a 'yes sir' on your tongue for him, or you'll be lookin' for work somewhere else," Luke had snapped at a hand named Hendry, a new man who'd only been at the ranch a few months. Hendry had glared at Luke, but apparently he'd thought holding his tongue was easier than finding a new job, and Stone had slipped away before either of them knew he'd been there. Yet he had to wonder if tongues would be wagging in the bunkhouse that night, as the hands speculated on why their foreman seemed so determined to defend their boss, no matter what.

Fortunately, it seemed what Stone had revealed about his parents had generated far more talk than what Luke had said in his defense, so their secret was still safe, at least for now. He was relieved about that, although there was a small part of him that wondered what would have happened if everything had come out. If they'd been run out of town, could they actually be together, or would Luke end up hating him? For all that Luke protested Copper Lake was just a place and not his home, he cared for every aspect of it as if it was his own, and he took pride in its prosperity. The laws of society meant nothing compared to what a man felt like he owned in his heart.

Thoughts of Luke continued to occupy him until they arrived at the ranch. As he pulled up, Little Sam jumped down and began unloading the supplies, and Stone left him to it, deciding to head to the stable to check on Raider. He'd not been up on the big stallion since he'd been thrown, and he decided it was past time to get back in the saddle. He hadn't been leery of riding again; he'd just had an overprotective nanny named Luke who raised a fuss every time he mentioned it, claiming it was too soon and he risked hurting himself worse if Raider threw him again.

He entered the cool, dim stable and headed toward Raider's stall. Raider was glad to see him, and Stone stroked his nose fondly. "'Least there ain't nothin' complicated about you, is there?" he asked, and Raider snorted and nudged Stone in an obvious demand for a treat.

A few minutes later, Luke marched into the stables wearing a thunderous expression. He headed to Mist's stall, not seeming to notice Stone at first, but when he did, he attempted to erase the signs of anger on his face, although not very successfully.

"Get everything you needed in town?" he asked, sounding more casual than he looked.

Stone raised a brow and crossed his arms over his chest. "Yeah, but I'm thinkin' that whatever you got goin' on here is a lot more interestin'. What happened?"

For a moment, Luke tried a "who, me?" look, but then he grimaced, as if he realized he wouldn't be let off the hook so easily. "I heard some of the hands talkin' about this place bein' cursed. They couldn't even keep the story straight. One minute, Priss has come back to haunt the place because she don't like how it's bein' run, and the next, you cast some kind of Indian curse on it because you hate white men."

"What?" Stone stared, wondering if Luke was joking, but the expression on his face told Stone he was serious. "Why in the hell would they think such a thing? Has somebody been seein' ghosts?"

"They were talkin' about what's been happenin' lately," Luke explained. "Like no one's ever had a run of bad luck before."

Stone didn't believe in ghosts or curses or any of that nonsense, but he'd met plenty of people over the years who did. One cowboy swore he had to put on his left boot before his right one to ward off scorpions, and another old hand said the ghosts of cowboys who died on the trail could be seen riding across the sky at night, chasing falling stars like stray cattle. They wouldn't listen to anyone talking sense, because they believed it was true, and that was all that mattered to them.

Superstitions like that were harmless, but talking about the ranch being haunted or cursed wasn't; soon the hands would start getting spooked over the least little thing that went wrong and take it as a sign, and then they'd spend more time looking over their shoulders than doing their work. Some might even get scared enough to quit, and that could spell the end of the ranch. They needed hands to do the work; he and Luke couldn't run the whole place by themselves, and if Copper Lake got a bad reputation, they wouldn't be able to hire replacements.

"If I knew an Indian curse, I sure as hell wouldn't curse my own damned ranch," he snarled, scowling darkly. "Why do folks always have to find somethin' or someone to blame things on? We can't even tell them not to talk, because then they'd say we're hidin' somethin'."

"Yeah." Luke shook his head, looking glum. "I reckon all we can do is set a good example and show we ain't worried or scared, and maybe it'll die down if nothin' else really bad happens for a while."

Stone thought that over, frustrated by the situation, but he couldn't see any other option either, and he nodded slowly. "Yeah, I guess that's all we can do."

A horrid, loud groaning sound from outside made both of them whirl around, and alarm quickly turned to fear as the groan escalated into a high-pitched shriek. Stone had heard it before in wind storms when trees were being bent beyond their limits, and before his mind caught up with his body, he ran outside, arriving in time to watch as the massive wooden water tank holding all the water they used for the house and stables leaned crazily on its fifteen foot wooden posts like a drunken man staggering on his legs. The wind was blowing hard and steady, and finally one of the posts snapped, sending the wooden tank crashing to the ground.

Thousands of gallons of water washed over the ground like a flash flood and flowing downhill toward the lower pasture. Broken bits of wood and twisted pieces of the metal that had been used to lash the planks of the tank together were mixed in, and the hands who had been working outside scrambled to get out of the way before they were caught up in the rush of water.

Stone forced himself to move, running toward the side of the stable that overlooked the pasture. Hopefully none of the cattle were grazing too close on that side, or they'd be swept up by the water or hit with the debris.

"Oh thank God." He skidded to a stop when he saw that none of the hands or the cattle—especially the precious calves that would be going to market in the fall—were in the path of destruction. The water washed away into the dry earth, leaving broken bits of the tank in its path.

Luke came running up and stopped beside him, surveying the damage with visible dismay, and all he could say was "Oh, *hell*."

Stone stared at the wreckage, a horrified sort of numbness washing over him. He didn't know whether to scream or walk away from everything in defeat. If he'd been a different type of man, he might've started believing Priss really had come back to haunt him.

His pa would've given up, and that thought made him square his shoulders and turn to Luke. "I didn't see nobody get caught in that, but we should round up the hands and make sure no one was hurt. Then I want to talk to every hand that saw it happen. I can't believe it just went over in the wind like that."

Luke stared at Stone blankly for a moment, but then he seemed to shake off the shocked daze he was in and nodded. "I'm on it. You're right, it's hard to believe. We check that tank at least once a year to make sure it's holdin' up all right. If it'd been showin' signs of weakness or rot, we'd have caught it before it got to the point of blowin' over."

"I'm sure you do." Stone clapped Luke on the shoulder. He was sure Luke was feeling just as put upon as he was, if not more. Even though Stone owned the ranch, it had been Luke's job to make sure everything on it was kept running and in good shape for the past ten years. Now things were suddenly going so wrong, making it look like Luke hadn't been doing his job, but Stone had seen Luke work, and he knew nothing could be further from the truth. No, it wasn't a reflection on Luke at all, but Stone was starting to feel like it couldn't just be bad luck, either—not unless someone was helping it along.

"This is goin' to cost us, but we'll get through it," he continued, as much to reassure himself as Luke. "I just want to make sure this bad luck is really ours and not someone else wishin' it on us."

Luke looked startled, as if the thought of sabotage hadn't occurred to him yet, and then his expression turned dark. "If it *is* someone else doin' this, they'll have hell to pay when they get caught," he muttered, confirming Stone's suspicions he was taking this personally.

"Yeah, if we can catch them." Stone nodded grimly. "I ain't goin' to go hurlin' accusations all over the place, neither. Let's just keep the thought between me and you. If it is someone else, I don't want them to think we're on to them. In fact, don't say a word to the men about it not bein' Priss's ghost or a curse. Let them think that way, at least for now.

If it's someone makin' trouble for us, they might get careless if they think they're gettin' away with it."

Luke nodded, appearing satisfied with the plan. "Good idea. I'll keep my eyes and ears open and my mouth shut."

"That works. So let's get goin'. Don't want the men to think we're lettin' the ghosts win."

By the time the sun set that night, Stone had talked to every hand in the place, but he wasn't one bit closer to determining if there was anything suspicious going on. None of the hands who'd been close enough to see the water tank topple had noticed anything unusual, and no one had been anywhere near it when it fell. That was a blessing in one sense, because it meant they'd only lost the tank, not hands or livestock, but then again, Stone wished someone had seen something that would help him figure out if there was more than coincidence behind this run of back luck they were having.

One thing he did find out was that several of the hands were worried a ghost was out to get Stone, and a couple of them had seemed nervous talking with him, almost as if they expected him to put a curse on them. Stone had held his temper, even though he'd wanted to smack some sense into them.

He hadn't sent for the sheriff, since he didn't have proof anything untoward was happening, but he'd told Luke to have the hands stack all the debris they could find in the stable until he and Luke could take a good look at it. If it wasn't just an accident, maybe something in the scraps of wood and metal would help them figure out what had happened.

Tired in both mind and body, he'd finally called a halt to things when it had gotten too dark to see. He and Luke went back to the ranch house for supper, and Stone was relieved to learn James was spending the evening with Agnes and her folks, according to Mary, who had seemed amazed and a little envious James had chosen to spend time with a girl far less pretty than she, but Stone wouldn't have wished his cousin on either of the girls. In his opinion, Agnes was definitely getting the worse end of the bargain.

He and Luke had discussed what happened, but they hadn't been able to come up with any thoughts about who would go to such extremes to mess with the ranch, much less why. Stone had gone to bed still worrying over the question, but nothing made any sense. Who could hate him so much they'd wreck the ranch to get at him? In some ways, he wished if there *was* someone after him, they'd just challenge him to a gunfight. Stone far preferred an enemy he could see, to one that stalked the shadows like a ghost—especially if, by some horrible twist of fate, there really was one.

20

THE ranch was quiet and peaceful in the early morning light, but Luke knew appearances could be deceiving. Although construction of a new water tank had already begun, it would take a lot of time and effort to build it and refill it, and in the meantime, life was a lot more difficult and inconvenient.

Standing in the yard looking around at the ranch he'd called home for over a decade, Luke felt as if he hardly knew the place any longer. No, that wasn't quite right. Everything looked more or less the same, but it all *felt* different. When Priss was alive and Sarah was still here, Luke had been pretending, but in a passive way. He hadn't been interested in anyone, and being their decoy hadn't required much effort on his part. Hiding what he felt for Stone was a different matter altogether, and he was finding it increasingly difficult to keep up the pretense.

Part of his frustration was due to all the problems that had sprung up lately, and he knew that was coloring everything and making the situation seem bleaker than it was. Still, he couldn't help it. The ranch had seen hard times before, but this was different. Stone thought someone was sabotaging them, and Luke was inclined to agree. He didn't believe in ghosts or curses, but he did believe in deliberate meanness, having seen it in folks more often than he'd like, and the "coincidences" were starting to pile up a bit too high for him to see anything but malice at work.

All of it was starting to make the ranch feel less like home to Luke. He was willing to work hard and help the ranch recover from its recent losses, because those were problems that could be fixed. It might be expensive, time-consuming, and difficult, but the ranch's bank account was healthy enough to ride out a bad year. Luke still had no idea what to do about the problems with Stone, however.

A strong whiff of smoke brought Luke out of his thoughts, and he frowned as he peered around for the source of it. It wasn't trash-burning day yet, and anyway, that was done well away from the buildings in case a stray spark got carried by the wind. His heart sank when he saw a plume of black smoke rising over the stable and the telltale flicker of flames, and before his mind could recover from the shock, his body was in motion. He ran to the bunkhouse and began banging on the iron triangle Charlie used to summon the hands for a meal.

"Fire!" he cried desperately. "Fire in the stable! Get water! Get the horses out!"

There was a moment of silence as the triangle's sound died away, and then chaos erupted as the hands came pouring out of the bunkhouse, some without shoes or shirts on, caught in the middle of dressing. As he pointed frantically toward the stable, they rushed in that direction, most of them looking grim and determined; the horses were the most important thing to every cowboy on the place.

The back door of the main house opened then, and Stone came running out, his shirt unbuttoned and his feet still bare. He glanced at Luke, and there was no mistaking the despair in his eyes; without the water tank, they had only what water they could get from the troughs and the output of the windmill, which wouldn't be enough to halt a big blaze. Then Stone was past him, running for the stable, with Luke right behind him.

Men were already leading horses out, the animals wild-eyed with panic from the smoke and flames. Through the door, they could see the rear of the building seemed to be engulfed, and Stone grabbed Shorty as he started past with his horse. "Get the men on a bucket brigade from the troughs! We'll try to save it!"

Shorty nodded, handing off his mount to another hand and shouting for others to follow. Stone looked at Luke, and Luke knew they were thinking the same thing: Raider and Mist were in the very last stalls, closest to the flames. For all they knew, the horses could already be goners. But Stone set his jaw, nodded to Luke, and then bolted toward the stable, appearing determined to save them.

Luke ran to catch up, and Stone forged grimly ahead as Luke recoiled from the shock of heat when they reached the stable door. Luke paused long enough to pull his kerchief up over his nose before following Stone inside, squinting to see through the thick smoke; he heard panicked whinnying from the rear of the building and hoped none of the horses still trapped inside were suffering the pain of severe burns.

The smoke was far thicker and the heat more intense near the back, but Luke could see Mist was still alive, and he breathed a sigh of relief as he hurried to reach the terrified mare. The iron latch on the stall was hot and burned his fingers when he touched it; he hissed with pain, but didn't hesitate to unlock the stall and grab Mist's bridle, speaking soothingly to her as he led her out.

"It's okay, girl." He tried to reassure himself as much as her. "I've got you. You're goin' to be okay."

"Damn it!" He heard Stone curse, and when he glanced over at Raider's stall, he saw that a beam of wood had fallen from the loft overhead, one end ablaze and blocking the stall door. Stone whipped off his shirt and wrapped it around the unburned part of the wood, using it to pull the beam away from the door.

Luke wavered, but only for a moment. He steered Mist toward the door and slapped her rump; she whinnied loudly and sped out of the stables as fast as she could. Luke watched long enough to make sure she made it out safely before turning back, intending to help Stone rescue Raider.

He saw a shadowy form moving off to one side, and he peered through the smoke, wondering if one of the hands had gotten pinned or been overcome by the smoke. Quickly, he headed toward the movement, but he stopped short when he got close enough to see the man wasn't caught or injured.

No, the damned fool was dragging lumber *to the flames*! Luke was about to run over and demand to know what the hell he was doing, but then the pieces fell into place in his head. That lumber was from the water tank, and if someone wanted to see it burn, that probably meant they were trying to cover up something.

He edged closer, wanting to get a look at the man's face, and somehow, he wasn't surprised to discover it was that bastard, Hendry, who'd been bad-mouthing Stone to the other hands and trying to stir up trouble by telling them how wrong it was for honest white men to work for a red-skinned savage. Luke had threatened to fire Hendry over it, and Shorty had been helping him keep an ear out in case Hendry started up again. But Hendry hadn't uttered a peep since, not seeming eager to lose his job, and now Luke had a damned good suspicion as to why.

There was an ominous groaning creak from overhead, audible even over the flames and the shouts of the hands who were getting the last horses out of the stalls closer to the doors. He whirled to shout a warning to Stone, just in time to see him slap Raider on the rump, sending the big stallion thundering out of the stable like the hounds of hell were chasing him. Stone started to move out of the stall as well, but he wasn't quite fast enough. The hayloft overhead collapsed, sending burning hay and pieces of wood crashing onto the stalls below. A broken piece of timber caught Stone across the shoulder and head, knocking him to the ground as smoke and flames engulfed the entire side of the stable.

All thoughts of the traitorous man fled Luke's mind, washed away on a wave of sheer panic as he bolted toward Stone and dropped to his knees, reaching out to shake Stone's shoulders. But even though the timber wasn't that large, it had hit Stone with enough force to knock him out, and Luke struggled to lift Stone enough to drag him out. His eyes were stinging, and his throat was burning, but he ignored the dangerous creaking that was getting louder and coming from everywhere, focusing on getting Stone out as quickly as possible.

When they were finally clear of the stables, Luke lowered Stone to the ground carefully and yanked off his kerchief to get a lungful of air. Coughing, he dropped down beside Stone, his legs giving out now that the rush of fear and panic was subsiding, and it was only a matter of moments later the roof collapsed with a resounding crash that echoed in Luke's ears like a harbinger of doom.

The other hands were busy trying to keep the horses calm, and Luke saw they had abandoned the attempt to put out the fire. Not that he could blame them, since it was obviously a fruitless effort. If the water tank hadn't collapsed, they might have stood a chance, but without it, they couldn't fight a fire of that magnitude, which Hendry had probably been counting on.

Groaning and coughing, Luke tore his gaze away from the ruins of the barn and turned back to Stone only to feel a fresh surge of panic when he realized Stone wasn't breathing. It was the smoke. It had to be! He didn't think the timber had hit Stone hard enough to kill him with a single blow, but he had no idea what to do to get Stone breathing again. Desperately, he slapped Stone's cheeks and then hauled Stone upright and pounded on his back, as if he could force air back into Stone's lungs that way.

He wasn't sure if it was the pounding that did it, but after few moments, Stone suddenly began coughing, leaning heavily against Luke as he struggled to draw breath. After a couple of minutes, the coughing eased up, and Stone wheezed, shuddered, and then turned his head to look at Luke, his eyes dark and pained.

"Raider?" Stone mouthed the words. "The men?"

"Raider got out," Luke assured him, trying to keep his hold on Stone impersonal until Stone could sit up on his own. "I haven't had a chance to do a head count yet, but I think everyone got out okay, and we didn't lose any of the horses. We were damned lucky."

Stone nodded and looked at the remains of the stable. Without water, there was no choice but to let it burn itself out and try to keep the embers from igniting anything nearby. Stone had to know that, but Luke had no doubt it didn't sit well with him.

"Damn." Stone's eyes were bleak, his voice a hoarse croak. "I'm glad everyone's safe, but damn it, Luke, this is gettin' to be more than I can handle."

"Yeah, I know," Luke murmured, watching one of the stable walls start to collapse. "But I think we can put an end to it. We need to talk with Hendry."

Stone coughed into his hand, then frowned in puzzlement. "Why? What's goin' on?"

"I saw him in the stables, draggin' that leftover lumber from the water tank toward the fire." Luke kept his voice low, not wanting anyone else to overhear, not only to avoid alarming any of the hands, but also to avoid alerting anyone who might be working with Hendry. "He was tryin' to hide something, and I'll bet my last dollar he's the one who started the fire."

"Damn." Stone shook his head. "We'd better catch him before he runs off. I knew he hated me, but I never thought he'd stoop so low." He suddenly realized he was leaning against Luke and straightened, his face and neck flushing. "Sorry. It looks like I owe you for savin' my life. Miserable as it is at the moment, I reckon I ain't ready to give it up yet. Thanks."

"I reckon now we're even." Luke was relieved when Stone moved away. It would have been too much like torture to sit there with Stone practically in his arms for much longer.

Stone staggered to his feet. "I reckon we are. Let's go get Hendry. But first, I'm gettin' my gun."

"Are you sure you're up for that?" Luke asked as he climbed to his feet, watching Stone with concern. "Hendry didn't see me. He was too busy coverin' his own tracks. Maybe we should wait until he can't knock you on your ass just by blowin' on you."

"Hmph." Stone glared at Luke, but then nodded reluctantly. "Maybe you're right," he conceded. "Besides, I'd probably just as soon shoot him as talk to him, and we need him to tell us if he's doin' this on his own and why."

"My gut says he's takin' orders." Luke unknotted his kerchief so he could wipe soot off his sweaty face. "If not, then he's got more hatred for Indians than anyone I've ever seen, but if that's his problem, I'd think he'd just go ahead and shoot you instead of doin' all this."

"Yeah." Stone ran a hand through his hair, but before he could say anything more, they were interrupted by Shorty, who ran up, red-faced and breathless.

"We accounted for all the horses and the hands," he said, wheezing a little. "Sorry about the stable, boss. There wasn't enough water to stop it, but we didn't let it spread." He looked at Stone with concern. "You okay, Mr. Harrison? Looks like you took a beatin'."

"Fine. I had a little trouble, but Luke got me out. You all did a great job, Shorty. I owe every hand here for what they've done, and you can believe I'm goin' to show my appreciation. Otherwise we might've lost everything."

"We need to get the horses settled, and then someone's got to go to town and buy some supplies." Luke pushed his hat back on his head. "We've got to replace the feed and the hay, and we've got to start rebuildin' the stable as soon as possible. We might need to hire some more men, if anyone in town's lookin' for work. Otherwise, we're goin' to be spread pretty thin until the tank and the stables are rebuilt."

As much as he hated to admit it, Luke was starting to feel overwhelmed, but he would be damned if he let whoever was behind this win. It would take a lot of work and manpower, but they'd get the rebuilding done, and then maybe life would start getting back to normal.

"Shorty, you've got a good head on you," Stone said. "I'd like you to take Little Sam, Brent, and Dave and go into town with the buckboard. Tell Mr. Stephens what happened and get all the hay and feed he's got to spare. Then go by the mill and tell Mr. Williams thanks for the rush on the wood for the tank, but we're goin' to need the timber for a new stable instead, so we'll need more for the tank. Last, please stop by the post office and put up a sign sayin' we're hirin'. Can

I trust you to manage all that? Me and Luke have a lot to do here, so I really need your help."

Shorty drew himself up to his full six and a half feet. "Yeah, boss, I can do it." He ran off, obviously pleased to be given the responsibility.

Stone looked at Luke. "I hope you don't mind me steppin' on your toes like that, but I do need you here. We need to round up Hendry before he can do any more damage."

"It ain't unheard of for bosses to tell their hands what to do," Luke said dryly.

"True, but normally you'd be the only one I'd trust with all that. Right now, though, I don't trust much of anyone besides you, the men who've been here for years, and the men I know well. We can't take much more of this, and we're goin' to stop it, one way or another."

"I ain't in a trustin' frame of mind myself," Luke agreed, glancing around at the hands. He knew it was unlikely most of them were in league with Hendry, but it was impossible to know whom he could trust beyond the hands who had worked at Copper Lake for longer than a couple of years. The newer ones were all on his suspect list until he had proof they didn't deserve to be. "Let's go inside and rest a minute, and then we'll talk to Hendry and get some answers."

"Right." Stone started back toward the house, wincing as he stepped on a rock with his bare foot. "I'll want my boots too. And not just so I can use them to kick his ass up between his ears."

"You need more'n your boots," Luke muttered, glancing sidelong at Stone, who was half-naked and covered in sweat and soot.

Stone nodded, looking a little sheepish. "I ran when I heard you ringin'. I didn't stop to worry about much else." He looked down at himself. "I suppose I don't look too intimidatin' like this."

"That ain't the word that comes to mind." Luke kept his eyes fixed straight ahead as they walked toward the house, but he could feel Stone's gaze on him.

"I'll wash in the lake later," Stone said. "I guess for now, we'll have to make do with what we can get out of the pump. I'm just glad Dandy Jim decided a lack of plumbin' offends his sensibilities and took himself off to the hotel in town."

"That's the only good thing to come out of this whole mess." Luke grimaced, wishing there was a way to keep James in town permanently.

"I suppose I should wash before he decides to stop by for a visit." Stone mounted the steps and entered the kitchen, heading to the sink to prime the pump. "Let's talk to a couple of other hands before going after Hendry, just so he doesn't suspect we're comin' after him in particular."

"Good idea." Luke nodded, standing out of the way while Stone dipped his hands into the water, and turning his attention elsewhere. The last thing he needed right now was to watch rivulets of water streaming along Stone's bronzed skin.

Fortunately, Stone didn't dawdle. He cleaned up quickly and dried off. "I'll go change clothes while you wash. Then I'll start coffee, and we can figure out who to go after first. That work for you?"

"Yes, sir, it does," Luke replied, keeping his eyes averted as he moved toward the sink. It was bad enough when Stone was sooty; it would be worse now that he was clean.

Stone moved away from the sink, but then he stopped. "Luke," he said softly, and Luke heard him sigh. "Ah, never mind. I'll be back shortly." With that, he heard Stone leave the kitchen and the creak of the stairs as he went to his room.

As soon as he was alone, Luke released a long, slow breath and leaned heavily against the sink for a moment, feeling as if the weight of the world were resting on his shoulders. The ranch was falling apart, they had a traitor in their midst, and he was forced to keep his distance from the one person he wanted to be closest to. Life needed to get a lot better soon, or else he was going to have to consider some serious changes, because he couldn't keep on like this.

Mustering his strength and resolve, he pushed upright and primed the pump. They had a traitor to find, and he hoped stopping Hendry and whoever was working with him would mean the end of this string of disasters once and for all.

21

"No, SIR, I didn't see nothin'. I was in the middle of puttin' on my boots, and I come runnin' out with everyone else."

Stone looked at the grizzled hand sitting across from him at the table and nodded. Deke Jones was an old-timer who'd apparently been on the ranch since before Priss inherited it from her pa, and neither Stone nor Luke suspected him of any connection to Hendry. But that, he hoped, would make Hendry and whoever he might be working with relax and keep them off their guard.

"We didn't figure you did." Stone gave the older man a tired smile. "We ain't lookin' to blame no one. I just want to make sure that what happened don't never happen again."

"Sure." Deke seemed to accept that reasoning. "We're just havin' a run of powerful bad luck. Happens sometimes. Been years I seen where ain't nothin' gone right and years where nothin' gone wrong. Just happens that way."

"Yeah. I just wish we weren't havin' the bad one this year," Stone muttered. "Thanks, Deke. Ask Charlie to come here when you get back to the bunkhouse, will you? We want to talk to everyone. And thanks for your help in tryin' to save the stable. Would've been worse if you and the others hadn't worked so hard to save the horses."

"Yes, sir." Deke rose from the table, nodded to Stone and Luke, and left the kitchen.

Stone waited until the door closed behind him before turning his attention to Luke. "What do you think? Charlie, then Hendry? Or should we talk to a couple more first?"

"Just Charlie," Luke replied, his expression turning grim. "I don't know about you, but I'm ready to get to the real questions."

"Yeah." Stone tilted his head to one side and rubbed his neck to relieve the knots of pure tension. He couldn't believe that only a couple of hours ago, he thought maybe he was being too paranoid in believing someone could be sabotaging the ranch. Now, however, they were dealing with yet another disaster, and this time, Luke had seen who was behind it. Sure, maybe Hendry had a good reason for dragging the wood from the tank over to make sure it burned in the fire, but Stone wouldn't bet a plug nickel on it.

The biggest questions were why he'd done it and who else might be in on it with him, and Stone had to admit he'd be just as happy to beat the information out of Hendry as ask him for it. He was feeling every bit the savage Nelson had called him, and he was struggling to keep his temper in check.

The losses were bad enough, but Stone couldn't figure out why anyone would want to do something so terrible, not just to him, but to the people who depended on the ranch for their living. If someone held a grudge against Stone, why not just shoot him and be done with it? Why destroy a whole ranch? They needed answers, and he understood Luke's impatience to get them. After all, Luke's ties to the ranch ran far deeper than Stone's did.

He looked at Luke, seeing the unhappiness on his face. Oh sure, he had no reason to jump with joy with all the recent disasters, but it was the root cause of why Luke had been so miserable the last few months that made Stone ache. It was his fault, and he knew it, and he wanted so much to do something to make it better. But he wasn't even sure if that was possible anymore. Had he hurt Luke so badly Luke would just push him away if he reached out now?

And he did want to reach out. The ranch and his responsibility to it meant a lot to him, but so did Luke. Luke had stood by him through all this, helped him keep things together, even saved his life, and all Stone had done was keep him at a distance neither of them really wanted. He thought his reasons for doing it still mattered, because he couldn't stand it if anything happened to Luke because of him or if Luke got tired of him and left. But life was short and fragile, as he'd been reminded today, and he felt he was being unfair to Luke. Once they got this matter with Hendry cleared up, he was going to square things with Luke, and they were going to talk. He'd tell Luke how he felt, and if Luke didn't want him any longer, he'd just have to take it and let Luke go. Somehow.

He pushed back his chair and stood. "You want some more coffee?" he asked, heading toward the stove. He didn't want more, but he was going to drink it just to have something to do other than pacing around the kitchen like a caged bear.

"No, thanks." Luke shook his head and leaned back, his arms folded across his chest. "I've had enough."

Somehow the words had an ominous ring to them, and Stone turned to look at Luke, but before he could say anything, there was a knock on the door.

"Come on in, Charlie." Stone admitted the short, plump man and headed back to the table as the hands' cook entered.

Five minutes later, they let Charlie go after he swore upside down and sideways he hadn't seen anything, not that Stone expected any different. As the cook closed the door behind him with instructions to send Hendry to the house, Stone began to tense in anticipation.

He glanced at Luke. "A man can do some powerful stupid things when he feels cornered. I just hope he don't. I want to kill him, but I'd just as soon he didn't give me a reason to do it in the house."

"He ain't got a lot of gumption," Luke said, shrugging. "I've had words with him before, and he backed down right quick, but I guess that could've been because he didn't want to risk losin' his job before he got up to all the mischief he wanted to."

Stone nodded. "Just look out for yourself. I don't want him to decide takin' one or both of us on is his only option. Whatever his beef is with me, I don't want you gettin' hurt because of it."

Luke smiled, but it was a thin smile without any amusement behind it, and he patted the gun at his side. "Don't worry. I ain't got a hankerin' to die young. If it comes down to me or him, I'm goin' to make sure it's him."

"Good." Stone would have to be satisfied with that, although it wouldn't completely stop him from worrying. Then there was a knock on the door, and he stiffened. "Come in."

Hendry entered, trying to look confident and unconcerned, but Stone could see from the set of his shoulders that he was on his guard.

"Have a seat, Hendry." Stone managed to keep his voice even. "We're just askin' all the hands some questions to see if we can figure out how the fire started."

Hendry shot a look at Luke as he took a seat at the table. "I don't know nothin'," he replied, shrugging carelessly. "I came runnin' with everyone else."

"Did you now? Did you notice if anyone was missin', like maybe they went out for a smoke first thing?"

Hendry's eyes narrowed, but Stone kept his face expressionless. Hendry couldn't know what Charlie or Deke might have said, and since he hadn't been in the bunkhouse, he didn't know what the other hands had been up to. But he didn't panic. "Not so's I noticed," he replied. "But I don't notice much before I have my coffee."

"I see." Stone leaned back in his chair. "You don't smoke, I take it?"

"No." Hendry began to relax a little bit, apparently getting the idea they weren't going to ask him any really tough questions. "Never got into the habit."

"Yeah, I don't care for it myself," Stone replied. "So you didn't notice anyone gone, and since you don't smoke, you weren't out there yourself."

"Nope." Hendry smiled smugly. "Is that all? Can I go now?"

"Just one more thing." Stone kept his voice light. "Nobody saw you helpin' get the horses out or helpin' with the buckets. So exactly where were you?"

That wiped the smile off Hendry's face, and he glared at Stone. "You accusin' me of somethin'?"

"More like wonderin'." Stone tilted his head toward Luke. "Seems someone saw you in the stable, but you weren't near the horses or fightin' the fire. Or at least not helpin' to put it *out*."

Hendry's eyes widened, and he looked at Luke. "You sayin' it was me?" He pushed his chair back and leaped to his feet. "You're a liar!"

"Then why don't you tell us what you were doin' in the back of the stable." Luke's voice was admirably calm, but Stone saw his hand move to the butt of his gun. "If you've got a good explanation, why then, we'll let you go on your way. If not, then we might have to pay a call on the sheriff."

Hendry jutted out his chin and clenched his hands into fists. "I weren't in the back of the stable, and you can't prove otherwise." He was obviously determined to bluff it out. "It's your word against mine, Reynolds. If you bring in the sheriff, there ain't a thing he can do to me. And you got it in for me, don't you? Because I don't like workin' for no dirty, red—" He stopped suddenly, realizing what he'd been about to say, and his gaze flicked to Stone.

"Dirty, red-skinned Indian?" Stone supplied quietly. He already knew how Hendry viewed him, so he wasn't surprised by the insult, and it didn't mean much to him anyway, coming from a liar like Hendry. "Yeah, I know what you think of me, and no, Luke didn't tell me. I heard for myself. I didn't fire you because I believe a man can do a good job without havin' to like the man he works for overmuch."

Stone paused, glaring at Hendry, and when he spoke again, his voice was as hard as iron. "But I won't stand for a liar who endangers the lives of my men, their horses, and their livelihood. Now I got a question for you, and you can answer truthfully or you can lie, but I guarantee you, I already know you ain't smart enough to do all you done just for spite. I mean more than the fire. You done that to cover up somethin' about the water tank fallin' over, and it ain't much of a stretch for me to think maybe you had somethin' to do with the windmill breakin' and the cattle that went missin', too. If you confess like a man and tell me who put you up to this and why, I might let you go. But if you lie, I'm goin' to shoot you right here and now and prove it was you when nothin' else happens to the ranch."

Hendry stared at Stone, his jaw falling open in shock. "You wouldn't shoot me in cold blood! That would be murder!"

"Would it?" Stone drew his gun, pulled back the hammer, and leveled it at Hendry. "Maybe I'm just enough of a dirty, red-skinned Indian I don't much care. Now are you goin' to talk?"

"Don't be lookin' to me for help." Luke's voice was hard and cold. "After all you've done to tear down what I helped Miss Priscilla build, I'll just look the other way so I can say I didn't see nothin' if he shoots you."

Hendry looked back and forth between Luke and Stone and licked his lips in a gesture that betrayed his nervousness. He glanced in desperation at the door, as though he might actually try to run, but then he shook his head.

"I ain't takin' a bullet. I don't care how much money he's payin' me." He looked at Stone with bitter dislike. "You want to know who's after you? Well I'll tell you. It's your dandified cousin, James. He hired me and Colter to come here and get jobs before he arrived, and he told us to mess things up good. He wanted to run you off, and I guess he figured you'd leave if things got bad. When you didn't, he told us to make things worse, so we did. Colter even put a burr under your saddle blanket so your horse'd throw you, and we thought for sure that'd do it, but you're more stubborn than he thought."

"James did it?" Stone shouted, unable to believe that a man who'd claimed kin on him, even one as annoying and full of himself as James, would be such a low down, no good, back-stabbing snake.

"What did I ever do to him?" He looked at Luke in total shock. "Why would he do somethin' like that?"

Luke looked like he'd been hit upside the head, and he stared at Stone with wide eyes. "I didn't realize, but James must be who she was talkin' about!"

At Stone's bewildered look, Luke seemed to shake himself out of his shock and offered an explanation. "When she got sick, Miss Priscilla told me about her will because she wanted to be sure I was willin' to stay and run the ranch until her heir turned up. She didn't even know if you were still alive, so she set it up so I'd be in charge for a year while the lawyers looked for you. She didn't mention any names other than yours, though, so I didn't realize James Rivers was the one who stood to inherit if you were dead or they couldn't find you." He paused, glowering at Hendry. "Or if you either gave up the ranch or didn't prove you could run it right in the first year."

"What?" Stone was completely at a loss. He remembered the lawyers saying something about "defaults" and "codicils" and other fancy words he hadn't understood, but he'd been too stunned by the thought of having someone give him a ranch to really pay much attention to what they meant. He knew he had to make things work; it never crossed his mind he could fail, so he hadn't worried about someone else getting the place in his stead.

James stood to get Copper Lake if Stone gave up, and damned if the man hadn't come out here specifically to make that happen! Stone rose to his feet, not sure if he was glad or not James wasn't the one he was staring at down his barrel. "I want you and Colter to get the hell off my ranch! You ain't takin' nothin' that you didn't bring with you, and you should feel damned lucky I ain't puttin' a bullet in your skull. But you're a fool, and you'll get what's comin' to you eventually. Just make sure you go a long, long ways from here, because if I ever see your face or hear your name again, I'm comin' for you, and I will shoot you dead."

Hendry swallowed hard, looking as though he was afraid Stone might shoot him anyway, but he nodded and backed up to the door.

Then in a flash, he was gone, and Stone sat down heavily, unable to believe he'd been the target of so much greed and hatred. He'd known James was a dandy and a fool, but he'd never guessed James was so viciously evil. "I should've known. I didn't trust him, but I never thought he was this much of a snake."

"Me, neither." Luke watched Hendry's retreat with obvious disgust. "I thought he was just a lazy moocher."

Stone put his elbows on the table and rested his head in his hands, tired and depressed. He was angry, too. What man wouldn't be, given the wreck James had tried to make of his life? But mostly, he was tired of everything being so damned complicated.

"What do I do now?" he asked, not really expecting an answer. "I don't know if I should shoot him, beat the pure livin' daylights outta him, turn him over to the sheriff, or maybe all three."

"If it was me, I'd tell him I knew what he'd tried to do and march him right down to the sheriff's office," Luke suggested. "Spendin' time in jail would be a hell of a lot worse punishment for someone like him than just shootin' him."

"I suppose." Stone looked at Luke, taking in the features of the man who'd come to mean more to him than anyone else. Once again, Luke was standing by him through all the disasters and strife; it made Stone feel like he was almost as bad as James, taking from Luke all the time, when Luke didn't pressure him for anything in return. And here he was, locked in a prison of his own making, not knowing how to reach out to Luke and try to make it better.

He stood up and took a step toward Luke. "I can't take it bein' like this, Luke."

There was a sudden loud banging on the kitchen door, and Shorty stuck his head in, grinning broadly at them. "'Scuse me, boss, but we just got back from town. We had some good luck! We ran into the reverend when we stopped at the sawmill. The lumber came in for the expansion on the church, but when he heard about the stable, he said we could take it instead! If you don't mind puttin' the stable up in a different place, we could start rebuildin' right away."

Stone was torn between throttling Shorty for the untimely interruption and hugging him for bringing the one bit of good news they'd had in weeks. He raked his fingers through his hair, gave Luke a look of wry frustration, and nodded to Shorty.

"That really was good luck." He supposed the whole town had heard about the fire by now, which meant James had, too, and Stone wondered when he'd show his face. But they could deal with James when he returned. Right now, the hands needed all the good news they could get. "I suppose we'd better hitch up every wagon we got to bring all that wood in."

"I'll start roundin' up some men to get the wagons ready." Luke pushed back his chair and stood up. "We'll get the lumber while you figure out where you want to build."

"All right," Stone agreed. Maybe it would be best for him to do some hard physical labor before confronting James. Maybe that way, he'd be too tired to beat the hell out of the man the minute he saw him.

22

LUKE didn't hesitate to pitch in and help the men unload the lumber and other building supplies once they returned from town, throwing himself into the physical labor to help keep his mind off everything that had happened lately. He had been feeling beat down after the back-to-back disasters, but now that they knew the cause of it, he was hopeful the run of "bad luck" was about to end and life could return to normal at Copper Lake.

Well, mostly normal, he thought, glancing covertly over at Stone. Priss had entrusted him with the task of determining whether Stone was fit to run the ranch, and it hadn't taken long for Luke to decide to help Stone learn to be a landowner, because he'd seen that Stone would take his responsibilities seriously. Stone seemed to *crave* responsibility, in fact, and the more Luke learned about Stone's past, the more he understood why Stone seemed to need stability and a place where he could prove himself. Unfortunately, it was that need standing between him and Stone more than anything else, and he didn't know what to do about it.

He was brought out of his thoughts by a group of hands approaching him, all of them looking worried, and his stomach clenched at the thought of getting more bad news.

Brent was in the lead, and he looked at Luke anxiously. "Hey, Luke, me and the guys was talkin'." He paused, glancing over to where Stone was sifting through the rubble of the burned stables with some of the other hands, looking grim-faced. "Do you think the boss is goin' to give up on the ranch? So much has happened, and I know this ain't goin' to be a good year. Is the ranch goin' to go under?"

Luke handed off the lumber he was unloading to the young man who'd come to get it and waited until he was out of earshot before replying. "It ain't goin' to be the best year we ever had, no, but the ranch ain't goin' under. Miss Priscilla managed her money well enough that Copper Lake can stand a bad year or two, so don't you worry about that." He paused and glanced briefly at Stone, knowing he was making an assumption, but he felt like he understood Stone well enough to make it. "I don't think Mr. Harrison is goin' to leave. He's pretty damned stubborn."

Brent nodded, looking hopeful. "You really think so? Things have just been hard, and you know, folks was talkin'...."

Charlie, who was standing just behind Brent, spoke up. "He means that guy Hendry. Him and his buddy Colter been sayin' Mr. Harrison'll probably give up. He said Mr. Harrison's pa was a quitter, which is why Miss Priscilla inherited the ranch instead of him."

"Mr. Harrison ain't nothin' like his pa," Luke replied firmly. "Hendry and Colter have been bad-mouthin' him 'cause of his Indian blood, that's all. Mr. Harrison's a hard worker, and he wants to do what's right for Copper Lake and the men who work here. You ain't got nothin' to worry about."

The hands looked at each other, and Charlie nodded. "He sure is a hard worker. Ain't asked none of us to do nothin' he ain't willin' to do himself."

"And he ain't blamed none of us for what's gone wrong," Brent added, and then he rubbed the back of his neck, looking sheepish. "I guess you're right, Luke. It's just unsettlin', the thought of mebbe losin' our jobs and not bein' at Copper Lake. I like it here, and I don't want to go nowhere else."

After all that had happened lately, it was a relief to know there were men who were still loyal to the ranch and to Stone. That was good news, especially since he'd been wondering how much poison Hendry and Colter had managed to spread to the rest of the hands.

"If you can stick it out this year, I think it'll get better." Luke gave them a reassuring smile. Personally, he thought things were going to get a hell of a lot better now that James wouldn't be hiring anyone else to sabotage them, but he couldn't say that. "We're goin' to replace everything we lost, and we're goin' to keep patrollin' the fence in case those rustlers come back. We'll be okay."

Most of the hands nodded in agreement at that. "Well, I guess we should get back to work," Charlie replied, and with that, they returned to work. Before Luke could get back to unloading lumber, however, Stone spoke from behind him.

"I hope they weren't quittin'. I'd hate to lose Priss's men."

Luke whirled, startled to realize Stone had sneaked up on him so quietly, and he took a moment to recover his dignity before replying. "Naw, they were worried the ranch was goin' under or you were goin' to quit. They said they like it here, and they don't want to leave."

"Thank goodness for that." Stone pushed his hat back and braced his hands on his hips. "Especially since I'm hopin' things'll get better now. That bein' said, I suppose I'd best get back to the house and clean up in case James comes by." Stone suddenly looked grim. "I'm sure he'll want to gloat over the fire, and that's when I'm goin' to give him the bad news I ain't as easy to scare off as he thought."

Luke nodded, glad to receive confirmation Stone wasn't going to walk away now. "He ain't goin' to be happy, that's for damned sure, but maybe he'll finally hightail it back to Boston."

"If I don't shoot him first," Stone replied, and then he shook his head. "Never mind me. I'm just in a bad mood. There ain't much more we can do today. We can't start on the new stable until the mornin'. Might as well have the men knock off and rest up."

"Good idea." Luke removed his hat long enough to swipe at his brow. "You want me there when Dandy Jim comes sniffin' around to see the damage, or you want to handle him yourself?"

Stone looked at him for a long moment, his dark eyes seeming to soften. "If you don't mind, I'd like you with me. He might try to bluff if he thinks he's dealin' with the stupid Indian. I don't reckon there'll be anything said you don't already know, and I trust your judgment if you think I'm about to do somethin' stupid."

"I'll keep an eye out for that fancy rig of his, then." Luke wouldn't say so aloud, but one of the reasons why he wanted to be there was so Stone would have a third party witness in case things got ugly with James. He hoped it wouldn't come to that, but better safe than sorry.

"Right." Stone grimaced. "I'd best go up to the house and put on clean clothes that don't smell like ashes and burnt leather. You comin'? I told Mary to leave supper covered for us, since I didn't know if we'd be done before she went home for the day."

Luke looked around, waging an inner debate. There was still plenty of work to do, but he was bone-tired in more ways than one, and he didn't reckon it all had to get done in one day.

"Yeah, I'll be along in a minute," he replied. "I'll let the men know they can quit for the day, and then I'll be on to the house."

"Thanks." Stone gave him a small, weary smile before heading toward the house.

Luke watched him go, feeling the familiar ache of longing and loss that had grown far more bitter than sweet lately. As much as he wanted to be a strong, good man and help Stone no matter how difficult it was to stand back and love him in silence, Luke wasn't sure how much longer he could do it. Then again, maybe it would be different once James was gone and they weren't dealing with one disaster after another. Maybe it would get easier.

But there wasn't any need to decide today, and he headed off to let the men know they could call it a day so he could get to his own clean clothes and warm meal that much quicker. With any luck, James Rivers would come sniffing around sooner rather than later, and they could send him packing once and for all. As far as Luke was concerned, that would be the biggest and best improvement to the ranch of them all.

23

STONE stared down at his plate and listlessly pushed the food around with his fork. Mary had made one of his favorites, chicken and dumplings with peas and soft, melt-in-your-mouth biscuits, but his appetite had deserted him. He had too much on his mind between James, the ranch, and Luke, and it had his stomach tied up in knots.

He glanced up at Luke. The light of the setting sun was shining through the window behind him, casting reddish glints in his brown hair. Stone remembered how Luke's hair felt, soft and silken as it slid between his fingers. He wanted to touch it now; he wanted to give them both what they wanted.

Well, assuming Luke did still want it. That was the question.

Sighing, Stone pushed back his chair, rose to his feet, and carried his plate to the sink.

Luke's appetite didn't seem to be suffering the way Stone's was, and he looked up from his meal, watching Stone questioningly. "Thought you'd have worked up a bigger appetite than that after workin' all day."

Stone shrugged. "Guess I'm feelin' off," he replied, scraping his plate into the slop bucket. "Don't tell Mary. I don't want her to think I don't like her cookin'."

"I won't." Luke studied him more intently, concern blooming in his eyes. "Should I get Doc Wilson?"

"Nah, it's nothin' like that." Stone put his plate in the sink, and then he stepped back and shoved his hands in his pockets. "I'll just let you finish in peace."

Luke glanced down at his plate, seeming less interested in the chicken and dumplings. "I'm about done myself. I'm more tired than hungry anyway."

"I wasn't tryin' to put you off your feed." Stone wasn't sure why Luke had lost his appetite, but he hoped it wasn't because of him. "I just...." He looked at Luke and cleared his throat. "Ah, hell. I can't do this anymore, Luke."

The concern on Luke's face turned to alarm, and he pushed back his chair and stood up, facing Stone. "You can't give up on the ranch now! Once Dandy Jim is gone, things'll calm down. It won't be like this all the time."

Stone winced. Luke thought he was talking about the ranch, of course. He shouldn't be surprised; he'd made everything about the ranch, putting it before what Luke wanted and needed, so why should Luke think he meant anything different? He needed to explain and try to set things right between them.

"That ain't what I meant." He wished he was better with words, so he could make his feelings clear to Luke without messing up things even more. "I mean, I can't go on bein' so unfair to you. I'm judgin' James for what he's done, but I ain't one bit better than he is, am I?"

Luke shook his head, appearing puzzled. "I don't follow."

"I ain't good at explainin' things," Stone replied, wondering how he could say what he needed to and not sound like a fool. "I've been selfish. I've expected you to be here and support me, and I ain't given you nothin' in return except trouble."

"Well, that ain't true," Luke replied, frowning. "I got a place to stay and a job. It ain't like I did all this work for free. I ain't never thought you *expected* me to do nothin'. What I did, I did 'cause I wanted to do it, no other reason."

"No, not that." Stone wanted to growl in frustration, and he paced back and forth, agitated. "I mean that night, Luke. That night we went to bed together. I ain't been fair to you about that. I told you how it was goin' to be and expected you to stay. It's the most selfish thing I ever done in my life, and it's eatin' me up inside."

Luke regarded him somberly for a long moment, and when he spoke, his voice was quiet and deep. "You told me how it was goin' to be, yeah, but I don't recall you tellin' me what you expected me to do. Right or wrong, stayin' was my choice. Nobody made me do it."

Stone shook his head. Luke was a generous man, and it wasn't surprising he'd be willing to let Stone off the hook. "I didn't think you'd leave. Copper Lake is your home, no matter what you try to say about it not belongin' to you, but that don't make what I said to you or what I expected of you right. I didn't even listen to you. I didn't take what you wanted and needed into account. I can't stand it, knowin' I treated you like that." He stepped closer, holding out his hand to Luke, willing to beg if that was what it took. "Can you forgive me? I've felt lower than a snake since then, but today I realized how bad I could've made you feel. I never want you to feel bad, Luke. I want you to be happy again. I miss seein' you smile and hearin' you laugh, especially when the reason you don't is me."

Luke turned his gaze downward and swallowed hard. "I don't think there's much to forgive. I know you got your pa's ghost hauntin' you. You got somethin' to prove 'cause of him, and I wanted to help you prove it to yourself and everyone else and maybe lay that ghost to rest at last. But if you want my forgiveness, you've got it. I ain't goin' to lie and say I'm happy, but I don't hold nothin' against you."

Hearing that Luke forgave him loosened one of the knots in Stone's stomach, but he wasn't done, not yet. He gathered his courage and stepped forward, resting his hands on Luke's shoulders. "Thank you, that means a lot to me. But I want you to be happy. You deserve it, Luke."

For a moment, it seemed as if Luke was going to respond, maybe even move closer, but his gaze flicked to something over Stone's shoulder, and he stepped back quickly, extricating himself from Stone's grasp.

"Evenin', Mr. Rivers," Luke said pointedly, putting more distance between himself and Stone.

Stone whirled to find James standing in the doorway, an unreadable expression on his face. Stone didn't know whether he was angrier at the man for trying to destroy his life or for wrecking this moment when he and Luke might have been coming to some sort of understanding. He supposed it didn't matter either way; anger was anger, and he clenched his jaw as well as his fists.

"You no good, lyin', double-crossin', filthy snake!" he hissed, glaring at James. "You claimed kin on me, and all you wanted was to get your hands on the ranch!"

James' elegant lips curved in a mocking smirk as he strolled into the room, seeming unconcerned by the accusation. "Why, cousin, I'm hurt," he drawled. "How could you say such a hateful thing to me when I've been nothing but a perfect house guest?"

Stone's eyes narrowed. "Oh really?" He wanted very badly to wipe that nasty smile off James' face. "Wreckin' the windmill, makin' my horse throw me, destroyin' the water tank, burnin' down the stable. You call that bein' the perfect guest? Not that you got your soft, white hands dirty in the process. Your hired boys did the work, but you're the one who deserves all the credit."

"You have proof of all this, of course," James replied, still looking so smug Stone itched to punch him. "Otherwise, I can't imagine you would slander my good name in such a way."

Stone pushed his sleeves up. "You ain't got no good name. A man is only as good as his word, and yours ain't worth a pile of steamin' shit. Anything that happens to your name, you done all by yourself!"

"Again, I must ask if you have any proof," James replied, seeming unperturbed by Stone's aggressiveness. "I can prove it if you slander or assault me, and I doubt the authorities would be as quick to believe your wild claims without evidence to back them up."

Stone stared at James, unable to believe the man's gall. "Are you threatenin' *me*?" he demanded. "You think you're just goin' to walk away from this without a mark on you?"

"From where I'm standing, you're the only one making threats, cousin," James replied with an elegant shrug of his shoulders. "I'm simply stating what will happen if you insist on making baseless accusations."

"Well it ain't like I made this up," Stone snapped. "We caught your man Hendry settin' the stable on fire, and he decided lettin' us know you were payin' him to do the dirty work was a damn sight better than rottin' in jail all by himself."

For the first time, James' mask cracked, and Stone caught a flash of genuine alarm in James's eyes. "Men like that will say anything if you pay them enough." He was obviously trying to bluster his way out of trouble, but he sounded far less self-assured now.

"Or do anything, if you pay them enough." Stone was pleased at the way James was finally starting to show he wasn't completely confident. "But you know, there's the little matter of Priss's will. You got a reason to make me fail and to pay to make it happen, since you'd get the whole ranch by makin' me give up."

James' eyes narrowed dangerously as he stared at Stone in silence, and when he spoke at last, his voice was hard and cold. "Maybe Hendry did tell you I hired him, and maybe you can suggest I had a clear motive, but you won't do a damned thing about it, *cousin*. Not unless you want the whole town to learn your *other* little secret."

Stone glared. "And what little secret would that be?"

"That you prefer the company of men," James replied, pointing at Luke. "That man in particular."

A ball of lead suddenly formed in Stone's stomach. Somehow James must have figured out about him and Luke, or maybe he was just guessing, but he wasn't going to let James think he'd won. "You have proof of this, of course?" he asked, parroting James' words and tone. "Otherwise, that's slander, as I believe you mentioned."

164

"The rumor alone would be enough to ruin both of you." James' smirk returned. "But as it happens, I can support my claims with words straight from your own mouth, cousin. You do seem terribly concerned about your foreman's happiness, and there is that night you mentioned. The one you spent together in bed."

There was a sound of blood rushing in Stone's ears as white hot fury enveloped him. It wasn't so much the threat that James would expose him and Luke; it was hearing James mention that night, daring to sully it with his words and twist it into a tool for his own purposes, that sent Stone over the edge. He wasn't even aware of what he was going to do until he was suddenly looking at James down the barrel of his gun.

"Not if I kill you first." Stone pulled back the hammer with a decisive click.

"Stone, no!" Luke exclaimed, stepping forward as if to stop him. "He ain't worth it!"

"I ain't lettin' him ruin your reputation," Stone replied coldly, not giving a damn what happened to him so long as Luke was protected. "I'd rather hang and have the satisfaction of knowin' he didn't win."

James' bravado seemed to have deserted him completely, and he stared at Stone, paralyzed with fear, eyes wide like those of panicked deer. Stone snarled, disgusted by the man's complete lack of guts, but he couldn't take the chance James would carry out his threat. Slowly, his finger began to tighten on the trigger; whatever happened, Luke would be safe, and that was all that mattered.

"Mr. Harrison, please don't kill him."

The soft female voice came from the hallway, and Stone's gaze snapped over James's shoulder to where Agnes Wilson stood, her face white and her eyes full of entreaty. "Please don't," she repeated. "I heard it all, and what he did was wrong, but I love him!"

Stone blinked, lowering the gun because he sure as hell wasn't going to shoot anyone in front of a lady. "You love him?" he asked, staring at her, unable to believe he'd heard her correctly. "After what he's done, you can say you love him?"

165

Agnes nodded and blushed. "I knew he was full of himself and selfish, but he isn't all bad. I know it." She glanced at James, frowning. "He just wasn't raised right. Back east, some folks think it's all right to do whatever they have to do to win. He just needs someone to show him what's right."

Stone couldn't have been more shocked if Raider had suddenly come up to him and demanded wages. "You're worth fifty of him!" He shook his head in confusion. "Beggin' your pardon, ma'am, but a rattlesnake is still poisonous even if you cut off his rattle."

"Don't let yourself get fooled by some pretty trimmin's, Miss Agnes," Luke pleaded, gazing at her earnestly. "He ain't goin' to worry about makin' you happy, and you deserve better than that."

Rather than defend himself, James inched closer to Agnes, moving behind her as if seeking protection. Stone sneered, not surprised he was cowardly enough to hide behind a woman's skirts.

Agnes drew herself up, looking very dignified. "Thank you kindly for your sweet words about what I deserve, but the fact of the matter is, I know what I want." Her voice was firm and certain. "I'm twenty-four years old, and I don't have any real prospect of a husband around here, especially since two of the most attractive bachelors are already spoken for," she added with a smile at them both. "But I do love him, warts and all, as the saying goes. If you will spare his life, Mr. Harrison, I can assure you he will leave Serenity, and he will never breathe an improper word about you or Luke. I swear it."

Stone was at a loss, and he looked at Luke, seeing his dumbfounded expression mirrored on Luke's face before returning his attention to Agnes. "You'd marry him?" he asked, wondering if he'd understood her correctly.

"If he'll have me," she replied quietly. "He hasn't exactly asked me."

Stone shook his head. He didn't know what Agnes saw in James Rivers, since all he could see was a backstabbing dog who was lower than a horse thief, but Stone had never pretended to understand the way the heart worked. If she could marry James, even knowing everything he'd done, that was her decision.

"Well, what do you think, Luke?" he asked. After all, this was Luke's decision, too. "Should I kill him, or shall we have an engagement party?"

"I'd rather not see anyone's blood spilled." Luke was still watching Agnes with a blend of concern and disbelief. "Not even his. And not in front of Miss Agnes."

"I'll marry her," James spoke up quickly, falling on the suggestion with pathetic eagerness. "We'll go back to Boston, and I won't say a word to anyone. Just don't hurt me!"

Of all the strange things Stone had seen in his life, this had to be about the strangest, but he was just as glad to settle the matter without being arrested for murder. And James sure wasn't getting off scot-free, either; little Agnes seemed to have a will of solid iron, and Stone had the notion being married to her was going to either make or break Mr. James Rivers.

"Well, then, I guess we should congratulate the happy couple, Luke." He looked at James, his expression implacable as he holstered his gun. "But let me tell you one thing, you coward. If I hear a hair on her head has been harmed or she's suffered one moment of sadness because of you, I'll come all the way to Boston and blow your head off. Do you understand me? Any more dirty dealin' and you'll pay. Miss Agnes is the only thing standin' between you and me, and you'd best make sure she stays happy and healthy for a long, long time."

James didn't look too happy about that, but he nodded with the air of a man who saw the prison door slamming shut. "I understand."

"You'd better." Stone crossed his arms over his chest. "Now if you two will excuse my rudeness, I'd be obliged if you'd go back to town and spread your happy news. I'll have Mary pack up James's things. I'm sure he'll want to stay at the hotel in town until the weddin', to be near his beloved."

Agnes walked over to Stone, craned up on her toes, and gave Stone a soft kiss to his cheek. There was gratitude in her brown eyes, and Stone got over his surprise at her unexpected action quickly enough to return her wry smile.

"Let's go." Agnes took James's arm, and then she nodded to Luke and Stone with the air of a lady who was taking her leave of a perfectly normal social situation. "Good evening, gentlemen. I do hope you'll both come to the wedding."

"Wouldn't miss it for the world." Stone gave James a warning look, wanting to make certain the man realized if there wasn't a wedding, he didn't have a future. "I'm lookin' forward to it."

James led her out, his expression grim, and it wasn't long before Stone heard the front door open and then close again, and he turned to Luke, relieved to have that burden lifted at last, only to find Luke gazing bleakly at him.

"I've got to go, too." Luke's voice was low and pained. "I thought I could do it. I thought I could be satisfied with stayin' here and helpin' you with the ranch. I thought just bein' near you would be enough, but it ain't. I want to be *with* you. I ain't stupid. I know I can't tell most folks that I fancy men. Dandy Jim was right about that much. But I ain't got to live alone and in fear neither. Priss and Sarah made it work, and hell, even Miss Agnes got her man, such as he is. I want *my* man, too, one who ain't afraid to be with me no matter how risky it is."

Stone gazed back at Luke, the words making his heart ache for what Luke had been through and yet, at the same time, erasing the last of his uncertainty. Luke *did* still want him, despite what he'd put Luke through, and it was about time Luke got what he wanted.

He put his hands on Luke's shoulders and gazed into his eyes. "Are you sure it's worth it? Are you sure I'm really who you want?"

The bleak look on Luke's face shifted into a confused frown. "You think I would've stuck around all this time, tryin' to help you fix everything Dandy Jim broke, if I wasn't sure? 'Tweren't because of the ranch," he retorted hotly. "It's just a place, and I ain't takin' nothin' with me but my clothes when I leave 'cause I don't give a damn about *things* neither. I know what I want, and if it ain't here, I'm goin' to go find it somewhere else."

"It's here." Stone wasn't well acquainted with happiness, but he felt it now, a warm glow inside him like a fire on a cold winter night. Stone had finally learned it didn't matter a damn what anyone else thought. He'd rather have Luke than a hundred ranches, because he'd learned the truth: home wasn't a place. It was a person, and for him, that person was Luke. "Believe me, it's right here, and I ain't about to let you go off and try to find it in someone else's bed. You're mine, Luke Reynolds, and I'm yours." He pulled Luke into his arms and captured his lips in a deep, hard kiss.

Luke let out a startled yelp that was swiftly muffled by the kiss, and for a moment, he stood frozen, as if paralyzed by pure shock. But then his brain and his body seemed to catch up with what was going on, and he slid his arms around Stone's shoulders and parted his lips, responding to the kiss at last.

Stone gave a small growl of satisfaction as Luke kissed him back, and he took his time, exploring Luke's mouth and reacquainting himself with the way Luke tasted and felt. Then he lifted his head and stared down into Luke's eyes. "If that offer to share your bed is still open, I want to take you up on it. And not just for one night. For every night."

Luke stared up at Stone, looking dumbfounded, and then he scowled and punched Stone's shoulder hard. "I ought to kick your ass from here to Reno, makin' me wait all this time! Do you know how much time you've wasted that we could've spent in bed already? Why the hell did you wait until I was about ready to walk out the door?"

Stone flushed. "I reckon I ain't exactly the smartest guy in the world. I've been tryin' to tell you for a while now, but somethin' was always happenin' to get in the way. I was gettin' worried I'd messed it up so bad, you'd just pack up and leave."

"Well, I was about to," Luke grumbled, but there was little heat in his voice, and he rested his hands lightly on Stone's shoulders. "I reckon you *ain't* so smart if you ain't figured out a man stickin' around after bein' turned away and havin' a ranch burned down around his ears means he still wants you."

"Well, I ain't exactly experienced when it comes to someone wantin' me," Stone admitted. "And I'll probably still worry about somethin' bad happenin' to you because of me, but I can't take seein' you unhappy anymore." He rested his palm against Luke's cheek. "I miss your smile. I didn't even realize how happy seein' it made me until you didn't smile no more."

"I ain't had much reason to smile without you." Luke leaned into the touch. "I know you don't want nothin' to happen to me, but I could break my neck tomorrow gettin' thrown off a horse. If you waste your life worryin' about what might happen, you won't never live it and be happy."

"Yeah, I guess I finally figured that out," Stone admitted sheepishly. "So, speakin' of bein' happy, do you want to stand here all night jawin' about how stupid I am, or do you want to go to bed?" He was quite willing to listen to anything Luke needed to say to him, but he hoped Luke would prefer actions to words.

"Bed," Luke decided at once, and then he gave Stone a look. "I ain't done jawin', though, so don't think you're gettin' off the hook that easy."

Stone gave him a wicked smile. "If I'm good enough, you won't have the strength to jaw. Not for a while, at least."

"Well, that remains to be seen, don't it?" Luke gave a little snort of amusement. "You better be able to back up those big words, or you'll give me somethin' else to jaw about."

"I think I can find a better way to keep your mouth busy." Feeling better than he had in months—maybe even better than he ever had in his life—Stone captured Luke's hand and pulled him toward the stairs. The worst seemed to be past, and he was looking forward to starting over again with Luke. And this time, he intended to make sure Luke knew in his arms was the only place Stone ever wanted to be.

24

AS THEY headed upstairs, Luke kept glancing at Stone, still a little in shock at this sudden, unexpected turn of events. He had no idea what had prompted Stone's change of heart, and part of him wondered if he'd end up being rejected again in the morning once Stone had time to sleep on it and maybe change his mind.

"Your room or mine?" he asked once they reached the top of the steps.

Stone squeezed his hand as though he could see Luke fretting. "Mine. At least until we can pick which one we want to make *ours*."

"You sure about that?" he asked, searching Stone's face intently. It was foolish, maybe, to worry so much, especially since he'd just fussed at Stone about doing the same thing, instead of just enjoying himself for however long it lasted. He couldn't be casual about this, not when he was in love with Stone. For all he'd blustered about finding a man somewhere else, he knew that wouldn't be possible until he'd managed to get Stone out of his system, which wouldn't happen for a long, long time.

"I'm sure." Stone pulled Luke into his bedroom and closed the door behind them before looking at Luke somberly. "I know I ain't given you much cause to trust that I'm goin' to be there for you in the mornin', but I swear I will be. I ain't good with words, but...." He stepped closer and reached out to stroke Luke's cheek. "I love you,

Luke. I never said that to any man before, and I ain't goin' to say it to any man but you. No matter what happens, you're the only one I want, and I'm goin' to stick by you. Unless you decide you don't want me no more, and even then I'm goin' to do everything I can to change your mind."

Luke knew he was staring at Stone like a fool, but he couldn't help it. That was the last thing he'd expected to hear Stone say, and for a moment, he wondered if he was dreaming and he'd wake up to find out things were just like they had been for months.

"I've been stickin' by you, and I ain't goin' to stop now. I love you too, and I ain't leavin' unless you make me go."

There was a fierce light in Stone's eyes, and he pulled Luke against him, wrapping his arms around Luke and holding him tightly. "I'd marry you if I could, but since that ain't possible, I'm willin' to put it in writin' that you're my partner, if you want."

"I don't need nothin' in writin'," Luke replied, wrapping his arms around Stone in return and pressing close. "I got what I need right here. Just don't ever tell me we can't be together again, 'cause I ain't hearin' it."

"I won't never say that again," Stone promised. "Once I learn my lesson, it stays learned."

"Good," Luke replied fervently, pulling Stone closer. "Now how are you plannin' to make up all those long months of sleepin' in a cold, lonely bed to me?"

"Well, how about I let you do anything you want to me?" Stone asked with a slow, sexy smile. "Or I can do anything you want to you. I ain't particular, so long as it makes you happy."

Luke studied him for a moment, considering the options. Although he hadn't been waiting for Stone to come around since he wasn't hopeful that would ever happen, he had been loyal for months, and he thought maybe it was time for a little recompense.

"It'd make me right happy if you showed me just how much you do love me and want to make it up to me." He raised a brow. "Maybe if you're good enough, it might even make me smile."

"And if you don't, I suspect my pride's goin' to take a bruisin'," Stone replied, moving his fingers to the buttons of Luke's shirt. He unfastened them slowly and brushed the backs lightly over Luke's skin. When he got to the last one, he tugged Luke's shirttails free and eased the shirt off Luke's shoulders, baring him to the waist. Heat rose in Stone's dark eyes as he placed his palms flat on Luke's chest, caressing him with wonder. "You look good. Really good."

Luke hummed softly with pleasure, closing his eyes briefly as he savored Stone's long-desired touch; he had worn the memories of their one night together thin. Reality was so much better.

"You feel good," he murmured, arching into the caresses in a silent hint for more.

Stone chuckled softly, continuing to stroke Luke's skin. He caressed the muscles of Luke's shoulders, and then down over his chest again before circling his thumbs over Luke's nipples teasingly. "Do you like that?"

Luke gasped and nodded, grasping Stone's shoulders tightly to keep himself upright. He hadn't felt much like pleasuring himself over the past few months, and he knew he was going to pay for it now, getting wound up so quickly he wouldn't be able to last long.

"I like it a lot."

"Good." Stone continued to tease Luke's nipples until they were taut and aching, and then he moved his hands lower, slowly mapping each rib, then the muscles of Luke's stomach. Finally he moved even lower, his warm hand brushing over the hard length of Luke's cock beneath the tight fabric of his jeans. "Well, well, is this all for me? I feel like I won first prize at the county fair."

"Yeah, it's all yours." Luke squirmed at the teasing touches that were insufficient to offer any relief. "Ain't no one else ever goin' to touch me again but you."

Stone looked at him, an unmistakable light of possessiveness in his eyes. "Damn sure better not be. What I have, I aim to keep." He continued to tease Luke for a moment, and then he swiftly unfastened Luke's fly. "But I'm goin' to make sure you get touched all you want."

With that, he pushed Luke's jeans down his hips and drew in a breath as he looked at Luke's cock, wrapping his fingers around it and slowly stroking from base to tip.

Shuddering, Luke clenched his fingers on Stone's shoulders, unable to hold back a low moan; he needed this so much, and after months of deprivation, every little touch brought exquisite pleasure that sent a rush of heat through him.

"I want a *lot*," Luke replied, his breathing already turning shallow.

"You'll get it. But let's get you more comfortable first. I want to take my time makin' you scream."

He slowly walked Luke backward to the bed, reaching around to strip the quilt before lowering Luke to the edge of the feather mattress. He knelt, removing Luke's boots and socks and pulling his jeans the rest of the way off. "Lie down," Stone ordered, before pulling off his own boots and tossing them aside. "I'm ready to take what's mine."

Luke wasn't sure where all this aggressiveness had come from, but he liked it, and he didn't hesitate to climb on the bed and stretch out, putting himself on display. If Stone was going to tease him, he was going to tease right back, and he stroked his chest idly and shifted his hips to give Stone a good view.

"Well, hurry up," he demanded, giving Stone a mock frown. "Ain't you made me wait long enough already? You better get over here before I die of old age."

Stone huffed as he unbuttoned his shirt. "You sure are demandin' for a foreman." He stripped away his clothing as fast as humanly possible. In another moment he was bare, and he walked toward the bed, not at all shy about letting Luke see how aroused he was. Stone was bronze in the lantern light, lean and hard muscled, with a light sprinkling of black hair making him look even darker. "You're lucky I'm the forgivin' sort."

He crawled into the bed, moving over Luke and pressing down against him. "I want this to be good for you. If I get too rough, tell me to stop."

Luke laughed softly as he wrapped his arms around Stone, savoring the feel of Stone's warm, bare skin against his own; he had missed this more than he thought possible, and all seemed right in the world now that Stone was back in his arms.

"You can't get too rough for me, boss," he drawled, stroking Stone's back from shoulder to hip, wanting to reacquaint himself with Stone's body. "I've been wantin' you too much for too long to care about bein' gentle and slow. I want you to take me and prove I'm your man."

The warm light in Stone's eyes blazed into outright fire, and he swooped down, capturing Luke's lips again, kissing him as though trying to steal the very breath from his body. Then he pulled back, opening the drawer of his nightstand and pulling out a small bottle of oil.

Kneeling between Luke's legs, Stone opened the bottle and coated his fingers, and then he put the bottle back on the table. He met and held Luke's gaze as he touched the puckered skin at Luke's entrance, then circled his fingers for a moment before Luke felt him press harder, slipping one finger just inside.

"I seem to recall a certain night where I was wantin', and *someone* made me wait." The finger slid a little deeper. "You know what they say about gettin' what you deserve."

Moaning, Luke let his bent knees fall open, and he rocked his hips up, feeling a prickle of heat as his skin flushed with arousal. "Aw, damn, can't you pay me back some other time?" he pleaded. "Please, Stone, I need you. Don't make me wait!"

Stone smiled wickedly. "You'll wait until I say you're good and ready." A second finger joined the first. He placed a hand on Luke's abdomen, stroking him soothingly. "It won't take long, I promise, but I don't want to hurt you. Besides, I like seein' you like this, needy and wantin' and desperate for me. It's damn hard to hold back from just shovin' into you so I can feel you around my cock, all tight and hot."

Stone's words set off an explosion of pure, hot need in Luke, and he stopped just short of begging Stone to do *exactly that*, knowing it would be to no avail. But the image of Stone taking him hard and rough wouldn't leave his mind, and his moans turned to needy groans as he lay quivering beneath Stone's hand.

"I *am* desperate," he replied, a hint of a growl in his voice. "I need more'n your damned fingers in me!"

"Well, when you put it *that* way." Still grinning at him, Stone removed his fingers and picked up the bottle again, pouring more oil in his hand. He quickly coated himself before grasping Luke's hips, lifting Luke so he could feel Stone's cock nudging against his entrance. Eyes dark and intense, Stone eased into Luke's body, burying himself deep.

"Yes!" Luke braced his feet on the bed and rocked his hips up, wanting to send Stone deeper. The stretching burn faded quickly, leaving only the pleasure of being joined at last, and he clamped his hands on Stone's firm ass, urging him on. "Do it, make me yours," he demanded, his voice rough with need. "I ain't goin' to break!"

"You're *mine*," Stone growled, punctuating the possessive words with another deep thrust. "No one but me gets to take you. No one but me gets to touch you."

"No one else," Luke agreed readily, his toes curling at the pleasure of each delicious thrust. This was right and good, and after months of loneliness, he felt like he couldn't get Stone close enough or deep enough to satisfy him. "I'm your man, and you're *mine*. Ain't no one else ever goin' to touch you or take you but me."

Stone smiled. "Fair enough." He ran one hand over Luke's chest and then moved it lower, wrapping his fingers around Luke's cock again. "Now that we got that settled, I'm goin' to start makin' up for lost time." Stone pulled out almost all the way, and then moved forward again slowly, stroking Luke at the same time. "Is that how you want it?"

Luke heard someone whimpering and could scarcely believe *he* was the one making that low, needy sound. Stone was torturing him; there was no other word for it, but he couldn't bring himself to make Stone stop, not when it felt so damned good.

"*Yes.*" His voice sounded strangled even to his ears. "More! I need more!"

Apparently Stone was determined to kill him, because he began to move, but slowly, drawing every moment out until it was a torment. Not that Stone was unaffected; his skin was flushed, and a sheen of sweat made him gleam in the low light. But there was determination in his eyes as he leaned over and pushed in even deeper. Luke moved with him, matching Stone's rhythm, and his whole world dwindled to nothing but heat and need and the feel of Stone on and in him. Desire blended with desperation until he was writhing helplessly, gasping for breath and not thinking clearly enough to beg. All he could do was moan as he clung to Stone, the only solid thing left in his world.

Stone's control seemed to crumble. He was breathing hard, and he began to move faster, claiming Luke roughly, driving into him even as he stroked Luke's cock in counterpoint. "All mine," he groaned raggedly, his expression fierce. "I ain't never goin' to let you go."

The part of Luke's mind that was still partially functional agreed with that sentiment completely, but he was in no condition to voice it. The quicker pace was driving him to the edge, and all he could do was hang on for the ride. The pleasure-tension coiled tighter, his entire body grew taut, quivering as Stone took him to heights of pleasure he'd never imagined before. Then he fell, calling out Stone's name as ecstasy overcame him.

"Yes!" He heard Stone's encouragement as Stone continued to stroke him, wringing every last bit of pleasure from him. Then Stone groaned, his movements becoming more desperate, until he threw his head back and let out a shout as he came.

Utterly sated, Luke sank back against the pillows and managed to lift his heavy arms enough to slide them around Stone's shoulders, smiling lazily up at Stone. "I'm gettin' the idea you're a bit possessive. It's just a thought, mind you. I could be wrong."

Stone raised a brow. "I must notta been as good as I was hopin', if you can still think," he replied. "But yeah, I ain't much for sharin' certain things." Then he grinned. "But at least I made you smile."

"Well, I finally got somethin' to smile about." Luke rested his palm against Stone's cheek gently. "As for sharin', I don't reckon you have to if you don't want to. Keep on lovin' me like that, and I won't never be able to walk right again, much less muster up much interest in any other man."

Stone pressed his lips against Luke's palm. "Then I'd best keep lovin' you just like that." He chuckled as he drew back and collapsed by Luke's side with a heavy sigh, one arm draped across Luke's waist. "Even if it kills me!"

"Least you'll die with a smile on your face." Luke was unable to suppress a grin. He felt lighter and happier than he had in months, and he shifted closer to Stone, basking in the warmth of Stone's body pressed against his. This was where he'd longed to be since their first night together, and this was where he belonged.

He'd once asked Priss how she managed to stay in love with one woman for so long. She'd simply smiled and said it wasn't that hard when you were with the right person. He hadn't understood back then, but he understood now that he'd found the right man. He saw years stretching out in front of him, years filled with days spent tending to the ranch and nights filled with loving, and Luke wanted every last one of them and more.

Stone chuckled softly. "True. But I'd just as soon not die quite yet." He trailed his fingers over Luke's skin. "I have a lot to make up to you. And a lot I want to do, startin' with puttin' your name on the deed to the ranch, right next to mine. If we can't get hitched, at least we can be partners, right?"

"If that's what you want to do." Luke rolled onto his side to face Stone. "I don't need no piece of paper sayin' we're partners, 'cause you ain't never treated me like I'm just another hand, but if bein' your partner comes with special privileges…." He trailed his hand down the length of Stone's body and let it come to rest on Stone's inner thigh, smirking wickedly. "I ain't goin' to say no."

Stone's breath hitched. "I just want to make sure you're taken care of if anything happens to me." He gently caressed Luke's cheek. "I

178

want this to be your home. I know it ain't nothin' but a place, but I want it to be *our* place."

"Then we'll get that piece of paper." Luke straddled Stone's hips and leaned down to claim a lingering kiss, touched by Stone's insistence on making sure he was provided for. Then again, Priss had done the same for Sarah, making sure she never had to work as someone's housekeeper again if she didn't want to. "And we'll fix everything Dandy Jim broke on our ranch, and we'll make it good as new in no time."

"I'd like that." Stone gazed up at Luke, his expression tender, something Luke had never seen from him before. He knew Stone held the rest of the world at a distance, and he had an idea of just how lonely Stone must have been over the years, but now Stone had let Luke in completely, and he was letting Luke see all of him, with nothing held back.

"Me too." Luke leaned down to kiss him again, sealing the bargain. For all his teasing nature, he wasn't about to treat Stone's heart lightly; it was his greatest treasure, more valuable than any material possession, and he intended to take care of it so Stone would never have cause to regret letting him in.

25

"THERE you are, pretty girl." Stone smiled as Mist daintily accepted the carrot he offered. He stroked her velvety nose and drew back as Raider nudged him insistently. He chuckled and pulled an apple out of his pocket, giving Raider his own treat and watching as the two horses trotted off across the small pasture. Mist's belly was bulging noticeably now, even though it would be another six months or so until her foal made an appearance. In the meantime, Stone let Raider stay near her whenever he wasn't working; the big stallion seemed to sense the foal was his, and Stone didn't want Mist to feel lonely or neglected now that she wasn't being ridden every day.

There were five other mares in the small, sheltered pasture, all of them expecting or recently bred, secluded from the horses ridden by the hands. This was the start of the project Luke had suggested in the spring, and Luke had selected the mares and which stallions they would be bred to. He'd taught Stone all about the bloodlines and why he'd made the selections he had, and so far, things were going well. Only time would tell, of course, but Copper Lake Ranch was slowly changing from a cattle operation to a horse farm.

A gust of wind blew past him from the west, carrying a chill that proved winter wasn't too far away. Stone flipped up the collar of his coat and started back to the house. Hands were bustling about, leading their horses into the stable or cleaning tack while enjoying the last of the mild fall sunshine.

The new stables were bigger than the original ones, and they'd built them with extra large stalls to accommodate the pregnant mares. It had cost enough money to make Stone wince, but in the long run, he knew it would be worth it. As Luke had predicted, the price of beef at the end of the summer had been downright miserable, but they'd managed to scrape by and even make a tiny profit. Of course, that didn't account for the cost of the stable, the replacement of the water tank, or the repairs to the windmill; only Priss's foresight and savings had gotten them through that.

But they'd survived, and today was the one year anniversary of Stone's arrival at the ranch. It was the day when Luke would decide if Stone had fulfilled the terms of Priss's will and sign the papers that would tell the lawyers in Reno Stone was a fit owner. Stone would sign the papers that would give Luke half ownership of the ranch, as well as bequeathing the entire thing to Luke in the event of his death.

Stone hadn't bothered to hide the fact that he intended to make Luke his partner in the ranch from anyone. In some ways, it actually made things easier than letting people wonder why he continued to let the "help" live in the house, a nasty question James had planted in people's minds even before he'd found out about their real relationship. So Stone had made it known the bad luck the ranch had suffered left him short on cash, but thanks to a fictional inheritance from Priss, Luke had helped him out. Anyway, Luke knew more about managing the ranch than Stone did, so taking him on as a partner was only sensible. The townsfolk had accepted that, and any question about Luke's presence in the ranch house was laid to rest, hopefully for good.

Despite all the work of rebuilding what James had destroyed, dealing with the disappointing cattle market, and the stress of starting up the horse breeding operation, the last six months had been the best of Stone's life. At the end of the day, no matter how tired or frustrated he was, Luke was there for him, and they found comfort and pleasure with each other in the privacy of their home, shutting out the world and anyone who might judge them. Stone couldn't get enough of Luke, of touching him and kissing him and driving him wild with pleasure, and Luke drove him wild in return. They slept together at night and woke up next to each other in the morning, and Stone didn't know if he'd ever get used to the wonder of having someone who loved him, who he could love in return.

He quickened his pace as he crossed the yard, waving to the hands who called to him, but not stopping to talk. Luke was probably home by now, and Stone wanted nothing more than to hold him. They'd been apart almost all day, and Stone found himself hungering for Luke's touch.

"Luke?" he called as he stepped into the kitchen and closed the door. "Hey, Luke! Are you home?"

A moment later, Luke sauntered into the kitchen, shirtless and barefoot, wearing only his jeans; his hair was damp, and as he moved closer, Stone caught a whiff of soap. "Here I am." He flashed a mischievous grin. "'Bout time you got home."

Stone's heart beat faster, as it always seemed to do in Luke's presence. He didn't hesitate to wrap his arms around Luke, pulling him close and running his hands down the warm, smooth skin of Luke's back. "I was putting Raider out with Mist." He buried his face against Luke's neck, inhaling deeply his clean, beloved scent. "Mmm. You smell good enough to eat."

Luke slid his arms around Stone's shoulders and leaned into him, relaxing easily in his arms. "Won't bother me none if you want to take a little taste before supper," Luke replied, a teasing note in his voice.

One of the other developments over the past few months that had added to Stone's happiness was the return of Luke's playfulness. Slowly, he'd begun smiling, laughing, and teasing Stone again, and now, he was the same aggravating cowboy Stone had met on his first day at Copper Lake.

Aggravating, but also sexy as hell and tempting to boot. Stone chuckled and bit down on the junction of Luke's neck and shoulder, not hard enough to draw blood but unmistakably marking the skin. Lord help them both if anyone got a glimpse of the marks they left on each other, but they'd discovered they enjoyed playing rough sometimes and leaving small, secret signs of their pleasure. It meant they couldn't go shirtless around the hands, but Stone didn't mind that one bit. He reveled in knowing there was evidence of their claim on each other, even if no one else could ever see.

Luke shivered and tightened his arms around Stone, and Stone had grown attuned enough to Luke that he could already feel the telltale signs of growing arousal. "Are you interested in the main course, or you want to eat dinner?" he asked, nipping Stone's earlobe.

Luke's teeth on his sensitive skin made Stone gasp, and his arousal rose swiftly. "Dinner can wait," he growled. "Charlie ain't nearly the cook Mary was, and I think you'll be much more satisfyin'." It was true, too. Mary had gotten married three months before, and they hadn't found anyone to replace her, so they were eating what the hands ate or what they cooked for themselves. He'd much rather feast on Luke than eat Charlie's stew.

"I know how to satisfy you better'n anybody." Luke herded Stone over to the table, nimbly working the buttons of Stone's shirt every step of the way.

Stone went willingly, scraping his nails over the skin of Luke's shoulders. "You're right about that," he gasped as his hips hit the table. "So what are you goin' to do?"

"I'm goin' to get a taste of my own," Luke replied with a wicked smirk.

But whatever naughty plans he'd been about to torment Stone with went unspoken, interrupted by a knock on the front door.

"Oh hell." Stone gave Luke a look of frustration. He didn't know who might be at the door, but he knew they had to answer just in case it was an emergency. He straightened, gave Luke a swift kiss, and fastened the buttons of his shirt. "I'll answer. You'd best get a shirt on, just in case."

"Will do, boss," Luke replied, clamping his hand on the back of Stone's head and pulling him back for another kiss, nipping sharply at his bottom lip. Despite the fact that he was Stone's partner now in every way, he still hadn't stopped calling Stone "boss," partly for the sake of the hands, but mostly because it seemed to be his peculiar term of endearment.

With a cheeky grin, he released Stone and sauntered away, giving Stone a good view of his jeans-clad ass as he went.

Stone watched, entranced, until another knock at the door brought him back to reality. "I'm comin'. Hang on!" he called, hurrying through the parlor to the door. He paused, drawing in a deep breath, and opened it.

Two women stood on the porch, dressed in plain but decent traveling clothes. One wore a determined expression; she had dark hair and blue eyes, and while Stone wasn't good at placing a woman's age, she seemed to be in her late twenties, older than Agnes, but not by much. The other woman was possibly a few years younger with blond ringlets escaping from her bonnet and soft gray eyes that looked at Stone pensively. They each held a traveling case, and from the dust on their boots and the bottom of their skirts, Stone could tell they'd walked, possibly all the way from town.

"Can I help you, ladies?" he asked, wondering what had brought them to the ranch.

The dark-haired woman spoke up. "My name is Anna Ford, and this is Susan Evans," she replied in a dignified tone, although her accent was odd to Stone's ears. "You must be Mr. Harrison. Mrs. Rivers sent us. She said...." For a moment, her expression held worry, but then she straightened her shoulders. "She told us you and Mr. Reynolds might have a place for us. She said you'd understand."

Stone blinked in surprise. It took him a moment to figure out that "Mrs. Rivers" must be little Agnes, and Anna Ford's accent must be from somewhere back East. He wasn't quite sure what was going on, but good manners came to his rescue. "Please, won't you come in?" he asked, stepping back and holding the door. "I'm not sure I know what she meant, but why don't you sit for a spell and explain it to me?"

Both of the women looked relieved, as though they'd feared being turned away, and they didn't hesitate to accept Stone's invitation. He led them into the parlor. "Please, have a seat," he invited, hoping Luke would come back down quickly and help him figure out what was going on.

It wasn't long before Luke walked in, giving Stone a questioning look before turning a charming smile on their guests. "Evenin', ladies," he greeted them politely. "Can I get you anything? Maybe some water? Travelin's thirsty work, I know."

"Some water would be lovely, thank you," Miss Ford replied, and her companion nodded, murmuring a thank you as well, although her voice was so soft it was barely audible. Stone wasn't sure if she was shy or just very tired.

"Luke, this is Miss Ford and Miss Evans," Stone introduced them, relieved at Luke's quick arrival. "Miss Agnes—I mean, Mrs. Rivers—sent them to us. Ladies, this is Luke Reynolds, the ranch foreman and co-owner."

Luke's eyebrows shot up at that, but he refrained from blurting out whatever questions he had and went to fetch their guests some water. When he returned, he handed over the glasses with a smile and took a seat in his usual chair near Stone's.

"How is Mrs. Rivers doing?" Luke asked. "I hope married life is suitin' her well."

"Mrs. Rivers is a wonderful lady, and she's doing very well," Miss Ford replied quickly. "In fact, I have a letter for you, from her." She opened the case by her feet and pulled out a cream-colored envelope, offering it to Stone. "She said she'd explain things, but I suppose I should speak for us." She glanced at the other woman, who nodded, then looked back at them. "We worked for the Rivers family in Boston. I was the housekeeper, and Susan was the cook. But Mrs. Rivers—the senior Mrs. Rivers, I mean, Miss Agnes' mother-in-law— she...." Her voice trailed off, and her cheeks turned a bright shade of pink.

"She found out we are in love." Miss Evans spoke for the first time, and she raised her chin, apparently willing to say what her companion found difficult. "She fired us because she didn't want a scandal if anyone else found out her servants were "perverse," as she put it. Miss Agnes tried to put a stop to it, but nothing she said made any difference. We didn't know what to do, but then Miss Agnes came after us and told us she knew of a place where some folks might not mind so much, and if we cared to start a new life, she knew just where we should go. So here we are."

Things clicked into place suddenly, and Stone looked at Luke, raising a brow. "Well," he replied slowly, wondering just what Agnes had told the women about them, since Agnes had promised to make certain their relationship was kept quiet. "That does sound like somethin' Miss Agnes would do, don't it?"

"It sure enough does," Luke agreed, regarding the two women with sympathy. "As it happens, we could use a cook and a housekeeper 'round here, if you don't mind a more simple way of life than what Boston has to offer."

The two women looked surprised, then grateful, and Miss Ford reached out to take Miss Evans hand. "You don't mind, then? You won't hold it against us?" she asked, looking at Stone with a mixture of hope and fear. He could only imagine how difficult it must have been for them in Boston, if they felt their only option was to pack up and move all the way to Nevada.

"No, we don't mind." He looked at them with a serious expression. "That don't mean that everyone around here feels like we do, so I wouldn't go doin' nothin' in public. But my aunt, Miss Priss, lived on this ranch with the woman she loved for many years, and folks weren't any the wiser." He looked at Luke again, smiling wryly. "Ain't that right, Luke?"

"That's right. See, I helped them out a bit by lettin' folks think me and Miss Priss were sweet on each other when 'tweren't nothin' further from the truth. But it let her and Sarah be together in peace." He glanced over at Stone, his expression speculative, and Stone could practically see the wheels turning in his head. "Seems to me like maybe the four of us could help each other out." He rose to his feet and moved to stand beside Stone's chair, reaching out to rest his hand on the back of Stone's neck in a gesture that was more than friendly. "What do you think, boss?"

Stone saw the eyes of the two women widen, and he smiled, reaching up to take Luke's hand, bringing it to his lips and pressing a kiss against Luke's palm. "I think that's a fine idea. You're right smart, Luke, and so is Miss Agnes." He rose from his chair, sliding an arm around Luke's waist. "So ladies, what do you think? If you don't mind the speculation that might be attached to your names in relation to us."

The two ladies looked at each other. Susan nodded, a smile transforming her features into delicate beauty, and Anna grinned.

"Gentlemen, I think we could have quite a beneficial arrangement for us all."

"Then you're hired." Luke mirrored her grin as he slid his arm around Stone in return.

Stone nodded in agreement. "In fact, I have an idea. We have a foreman's house, but since the foreman lives here, it's been sittin' empty. How would you ladies like to have a place of your own? We can say we didn't feel it proper for two unwed ladies to live in the same house with two unwed men, but you know people are goin' to talk anyway."

"Really? Our own house?" Susan rose to her feet, her eyes shining, and threw her arms around Anna. "Oh Anna, you were right to insist on coming here! And Miss Agnes was right when she said it would be better!" She looked at Stone and Luke, smiling joyously. "Thank you both. I'm going to bake a cake for you tonight, and Anna's going to clean everything until it shines. Aren't you, Anna?"

"Yes, I will," Anna replied. She was less effusive, but her smile was warm. "You won't regret this, I promise. We'll get started working right away."

"Why don't you get settled first. There'll be time for all that later," Stone said a trifle gruffly. He was glad they were happy, but a little embarrassed by their gratitude. "Then we can talk about your salaries and such before you dive in. The house is out back. It's small but comfortable."

He and Luke carried the ladies' bags out to the house and left them already making plans for how they were going to make the place over into something beautiful. Once he and Luke were back in the house, Stone shook his head and looked at Luke with a wry smile. "Do you get the feelin' Miss Agnes is goin' to start sendin' a bunch of folks out this way?"

"Probably." Luke grinned, not seeming at all daunted by the idea. "And if she does, well, we'll find a place for them. Copper Lake's a big ranch, and we can always use a pair of willin' hands somewhere."

"True enough," Stone agreed. And they would. The world was a hard enough place, and Stone wouldn't make it harder for anyone Miss Agnes might send to their door. "Now let's see about that letter she sent us. Maybe it'll give us an idea of what we're in for."

Stone picked up the letter from the table where he'd left it and opened it. It was only the second letter he'd ever gotten, and considering how the first one had changed his life, he was definitely curious about this one. As he unfolded the pages, a smaller piece of paper almost fell out, but he caught it before it hit the floor, then started to read the letter out loud.

Dear Mr. Harrison (and Luke, whom I presume is reading over your shoulder),

First, let me thank you again for giving James the chance to redeem himself. Having now become acquainted with his family circumstances, I truly do understand why he has been so selfish and unkind. People here in the east are rather different from those in the west, but I am doing what I can to adjust their way of thinking. I may not have an effect on society as a whole, but I have made progress with James, as the enclosed bank draft will demonstrate. He recently came into an inheritance from another uncle, and I insisted the first thing he must do with the money is make amends for what he cost you. After having looked into the matter, I hope the sum will be sufficient to cover your losses in full.

James now understands the importance of having a clean slate— or if he doesn't fully understand it himself, he understands I believe it is necessary. For the moment, that is sufficient.

Lest you think I am unhappy, let me assure you I am content here in Boston. James' mother is a strong-willed woman who treats me very well, but she does have decided opinions on things, as I am certain Susan and Anna have explained. I hope you don't mind me sending them to you. When I heard about Mary's marriage, I was certain they could be of service to you, and that you, being kind and understanding men, would give them a chance. I'm rather pragmatic in most things, but I truly do believe love can conquer all. As it has for the two of you.

I hope to convince James to travel back to Serenity in a few years so I may visit my parents. I am expecting our first child, and hopefully by the time he or she is old enough to travel, James will be at the point of being able to offer you a sincere apology in person.

I will close this letter with best wishes for your health and happiness.

Yours,

Agnes Wilson Rivers

"Well, I'll be damned." He looked up at Luke and shaking his head in wonder. "She made James pay for what he did to the ranch!" He handed Luke the bank draft. "Maybe we can buy a few more horses for breedin' stock now."

Luke gazed down at the draft with visible amazement, and he shook his head slowly. "I ain't goin' to worry about Miss Agnes no more. Looks like she's holdin' her own just fine!"

"Sure seems like it," Stone agreed. He was grateful to Agnes for all she'd done for them, and he thought James Rivers was damned lucky she'd taken an interest in him. Even if James might not think so.

He set the letter on the table and returned to Luke, wrapping his arms around Luke's waist. "Now as I recall, we was in the middle of somethin' and got interrupted. Is that how you remember it?"

"I remember havin' thoughts about bendin' you over that table," Luke drawled, hooking his fingers through Stone's belt loops and holding him close and fast. "We got interrupted *before* I could get in the middle of somethin', so to speak."

Stone grinned. "Well then, Mr. Ranch Foreman, I suggest you get busy again and make up for lost time."

Luke proceeded to do just that, and as he surrendered to the pleasure of Luke's possession, Stone was grateful once again to Priss, and to Agnes, and to the fate that had brought him to Copper Lake. It had taken him a long time to get here, but he had finally found real happiness, and, even more, he knew his heart had found its true home at last.

ARI MCKAY is the professional pseudonym for Arionrhod and McKay, who collaborate on original m/m fiction. They began writing together in 2004 and finished their first original full length novel in 2011. Recently, they've begun collaborating on designing and creating costumes to wear and compete in at Sci Fi conventions, and they share a love of yarn and cake.

Arionrhod is an avid costumer, knitter, and all-around craft fiend, as well as a professional systems engineer. Mother of two human children and two dachshunds who think they are human, she is a voracious reader with wildly eclectic tastes, devouring romance novels, military science fiction, horror stories and Shakespeare with equal glee. She is currently preparing for the zombie apocalypse

McKay is an English teacher who has been writing for one reason or another most of her life. She also enjoys knitting, reading, cooking, and playing video games. She has been known to knit in public. Given she has the survival skills of a gnat, she's relying on Arionrhod to help her survive the zombie apocalypse.

Visit Ari on:
Blog: http://arimckay.wordpress.com/
Facebook: http://www.facebook.com/pages/Ari-Mckay/266185570179748
Twitter: https://twitter.com/AriMcKay1

Also from ARI MCKAY

http://www.dreamspinnerpress.com

Also from DREAMSPINNER PRESS

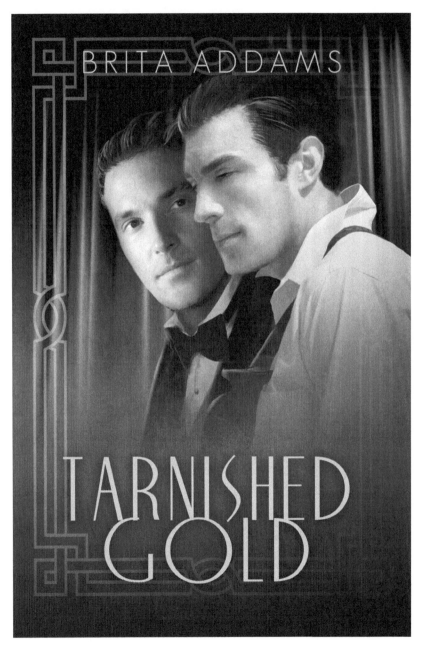

http://www.dreamspinnerpress.com

Also from DREAMSPINNER PRESS

http://www.dreamspinnerpress.com

Also from DREAMSPINNER PRESS

SHYING AWAY

Kate Sherwood

http://www.dreamspinnerpress.com

For more of the
best M/M romance,
visit

Dreamspinner Press

www.dreamspinnerpress.com

CPSIA information can be obtained at www.ICGtesting.com
Printed in the USA
LVOW010027260613

340190LV00031B/1804/P